Hard Knocks

Ruby Lang is the author of the acclaimed Practice Perfect series and the Uptown series. Her alter ego, Mindy Hung, wrote about romance novels (among other things) for *The Toast*. Her work has also appeared in *The New York Times*, *The Walrus*, *Bitch*, and other fine venues. She enjoys running (slowly), reading (quickly), and ice cream (at any speed). She lives in New York with a small child and a medium-sized husband.

Also by Ruby Lang

Practice Perfect

Acute Reactions
Clean Breaks

 Canelo US
An imprint of Printers Row Publishing Group
9717 Pacific Heights Blvd, San Diego, CA 92121
www.canelobooksus.com

Printers Row Publishing Group is a division of Readerlink Distribution
Services, LLC. Canelo US is a registered trademark of Readerlink
Distribution Services, LLC.

First published in the USA in 2016 by Crimson Romance, an imprint of
F+W Media, Inc. This edition originally published in the United Kingdom
in 2024 by Canelo. Originally published in 2016 under the pseudonym of
Mindy Hung.

Published in partnership with Canelo.

Correspondence regarding the content of this book should be sent to Canelo
US, Editorial Department, at the above address. Author inquiries should be
sent to Canelo, Unit 9, 5th Floor, Cargo Works, 1–2 Hatfields, London SE1
9PG, United Kingdom, www.canelo.co.

Publisher: Peter Norton • Associate Publisher: Ana Parker
Art Director: Charles McStravick
Editorial Director: April Graham
Editor: Traci Douglas
Production Team: Beno Chan, Julie Greene

Library of Congress Control Number: 2024934493

ISBN: 978-1-6672-0859-6

Printed in Faridabad-Haryana, India

28 27 26 25 24   1 2 3 4 5

Hard Knocks

RUBY LANG

San Diego, California

Chapter One

What a day for seeing the sights, Helen Chang Frobisher thought as she entered the exam room and took in the two mountain ranges facing her.

In the chair: the Alps. On the table: the Andes.

Of course, Portland never lacked for scenic views, but the two physically imposing gentlemen in front of her were a different story. They turned their boulder-hewn faces toward her and squared their chiseled shoulders. Alps stood up, but Andes just closed his eyes again. Clearly, he was her man.

Lacerations to the forehead and scalp, her brain noted as her heels clicked forward.

Andes was in a hospital gown. Alps was wearing a nattily tailored suit, but she doubted he was a businessman. Both men were too large, too craggy, too... panoramic, she thought briefly before putting on her doctor face.

They had been sewn up. The chart indicated minor contusions on the blond one she'd dubbed Alps. Dark-haired and dark-eyed Andes, however, had clearly taken a harder hit.

"Dr. Frobisher, I thought you'd be interested in meeting these gentlemen," Dr. Max Weber yelped. He flapped his clipboard excitedly.

She hadn't even noticed her colleague next to the huge men, so preoccupied had she been. He was practically dancing.

"Their minor car accident is our special treat!" Weber said. "Dr. Frobisher, I'd like you to meet – but wait, you probably already know who they are."

Max looked eagerly at Helen. Blond Alps, the one who wasn't white-faced in the bed, came slowly toward her. She looked way, way up into his eyes. Smarter than the average landmass, she thought, meeting his alert, interested gaze. He cleared his throat. "Dr. Frobisher," he said, "I'm Adam Magnus and that lump over there is Serge Beaufort."

He put out his hand, and she took it, her slender fingers immediately lost in his palm. Out of sheer bloody-mindedness, she was tempted to squeeze with everything she had. She took in his close-cropped blond hair and the Slavic cheekbones. His eyes were that color that everyone said was blue, but which she privately thought of as ghostly and white. But there was a disarming sprinkling of freckles across his nose – a nose that had been broken once or twice. *Farm boy meets gladiator*, she thought, trying once more to fit him into neat categories.

She caught another glimmer of amusement from him and ignored it.

A nurse had wrapped a bandage around Alps's forehead – Adam Magnus's, she corrected herself – and there was

2

a little blood on his shirt. Minor head wounds had a tendency to bleed a lot. Still, what the hell was wrong with her colleague, Weber? He was fluttering around the patients like a drunken Southern belle. She flicked her gaze back at Magnus.

"You should probably sit down, Mr. Magnus," she told him.

"I'm fine," he said. He was still holding her hand. "Dr. Weber and the nurses in the ER already worked their magic."

"Dr. Frobisher," Max screeched, "you don't know who these gentlemen are? Serge Beaufort is the goalie of the Oregon Wolves, and Adam Magnus here is the enforcer. He's the guy who makes sure everyone stays clear of our other players."

"That's great," said Helen extricating her hand. She moved closer to Andes. She still wasn't sure why she was here. Maybe something had shown up on a CT scan. "And the Wolves are…"

"They're our hockey team."

"Portland has a hockey team? No offense," she added, with a quick grin to the patients.

Andes barely registered her words. Alps quirked her a wry smile.

Helen felt her stomach tighten a fraction.

Adam Magnus was kind of gorgeous, if you went for the gigantic, lethal bodyguard look.

Helen didn't.

Well, not usually.

Weber was offended for the players' sakes. "Are you telling me you don't follow hockey? Doesn't anyone watch the Wolves in this town? Helen, you're Canadian, for God's sake."

"I don't follow hockey nowadays," Helen said, shrugging. "So... no one here is complaining of chronic headache, I take it."

She turned to the patient with a barely suppressed sigh. Head trauma was not her specialty – she usually looked at migraine and pain, but Weber had called her in on a routine mild traumatic brain injury case just because he thought she'd like to meet some hockey players. She supposed she ought to be grateful that her supervisor was the enthusiastic sort who paid attention to his charges.

Weber gestured for Helen to check the patient out. She ran through her list of standard questions, observing her patient's hearing, his speech, his memory. *Definitely a concussion*, she thought, as she wound down her exam. Interestingly, Beaufort's coordination and reflexes were still quite sharp.

Athletes, she thought again.

They'd probably both been playing since they were barely old enough to skate. That was how they honed that coordination and those reflexes that could grab bullets out of the air. That was how they learned the stick was an extension of their limbs. The movements were practiced and repeated and practiced until the procedures of each specific motor task, each grip on the stick, each flick of the wrist, each turn of the head, became etched in the

4

neuroanatomy. Her brother had played for a while. Fat lot of good that had done him.

She quickly checked off another set of boxes in her head as she completed Serge Beaufort's exam. He was murmuring in French, something about a puppy.

Oh, she was just enough of a snob to think that all those beautiful masculine reflexes could be put to something more interesting: ice sculpting, puppeteering, exotic dancing, Swedish massage. But instead, they chose to chase a little round pellet around the ice while wearing helmets and loose jerseys. It seemed like such a waste of flesh. She'd read a study that looked at whether athletes had a limited range of facial and vocal expressions because most of their concentration had gone into developing their larger muscle groups. She peered at Serge Beaufort's slack jaw again. His eyes were closed.

Unfair to judge the poor man right now, she thought. He had, after all, suffered a blow to the head.

But the mountain behind her, Adam Magnus, he had an imperturbable athlete's face. She sneaked a peek at him. No, that wasn't quite true. From a distance, he seemed impassive, but up close, he was hardly vacant. There was a restlessness around his eyes and mouth. His voice, although not animated, was deep and amused. So he chose to work in a profession where he used his body more than his brain. No wonder he had a smile in his voice. She'd cackle if she were paid handsomely to fill out designer suits and hit pucks. His buddies probably thought it was fine for him to gun his sports car on a Sunday afternoon and get into traffic accidents. They probably jeered whenever he punched someone, guffawed when he kneed someone in the groin.

There. She'd put Adam Magnus in his box and shut the lid.

God, she was a horrible, judgmental shrew these days. How the hell was she supposed to be a good doctor if she was already this cynical at the beginning of her career?

She finished up her notes on Serge Beaufort, aware of Adam's eyes on her. It was almost as if he could hear her thoughts. She felt herself redden, just a little, so she tightened her face and held her spine straight even as a small part of her failed.

It was this way all the time, now. She was angry, easily frazzled. She lost her concentration. If she kept this up, she'd be useless to her patients. There was no need to resent Adam Magnus. There was no need to be spiteful with everyone and anyone for simply being.

Except, she was.

Nurse Pham came in with the CT scan, and Weber left with her, chattering the whole time.

Helen took a deep breath. Her life was not terrible. Actually, it had been pretty charmed. Small-town upbringing in the Okanagan Valley, daughter of one of the town doctors, a house with dogs, wide-plank tables, and sunshine. She'd picked apples and done ballet. She had an older brother to assume the burden of being a perfect child. And she had been so stupid, so gloriously stupid, to take that for granted, to think that the whole thing would be forever preserved in the honey of memory, that her parents would always be fortyish, strong and wise and healthy, and that she would always return to find things that way.

She'd spent a few unhappy years in her teens at the San Francisco Ballet School, but that home – that beautiful home nestled in Canada – was the constant. When she finally quit dancing, college and medical school and residency went by in a whirl of work and studying and trying to sleep.

Everything until then had been good. Then her father's diagnosis came, just a couple of months after she'd started practicing as a neurologist. He'd been a boxer in his youth, and he'd suffered minor head trauma from a car accident a few months prior to diagnosis. But no one could say if either was linked to his growing illness, and it wasn't much use trying to find out. She'd handled that well at first, too. She'd conferred with her dad's physicians when she'd flown up to see her parents. Degenerative brain disease wasn't her specialty, but she'd researched treatments and gone about her life with the usual practical optimism that one expected from a doctor. Except that he'd only gotten worse. And now she could say that all her optimism was gone.

She was grateful that this patient was disoriented, so that he couldn't gauge how far her mind wandered during this exam.

She pocketed her pen and tried to smooth down the ridges of her sudden anger.

"How is he?" asked Adam Magnus.

His voice was unexpectedly close to her ear.

"We'll keep him overnight for observation," she told him.

"We have an away game tomorrow."

She wanted to flip him the bird.

"Dr. Weber will confer with your team physician," she said crisply. "But the fact is, Mr. Beaufort has had a concussion. He needs to rest, and air travel would exacerbate his condition."

He was only looking out for his friend's job, she told herself. No need to think the worst of him.

"Your turn," she said. "Sit down."

She should just go on her way, she thought. But for some reason, she needed to establish some sort of authority over him. And he did indeed have a head injury, minor though it was, and head injuries interested her.

"I've already been checked," he protested.

"Scientific curiosity. This isn't really an exam," she said, giving his sturdy chest a little push. "And you're not my patient, and I'm not really your doctor. Just call it an opinion."

"I guess some opinions are stronger than others," he said, with that glint again.

Mercilessly, she shone her penlight right into his laughing eyes. His pupils constricted immediately.

She went through the motions of an exam, but there didn't seem to be much to see, *just as he had pointed out*, she told herself. Alps was fine. More than fine. Sure, he had a few nicks and dents, but he was still solid and golden. She felt a little foolish for pushing him around, making him sit. She had just wanted to put him in a separate place, but it hadn't worked. For some reason, he made her jumpy. She felt transparent. She had needed to put him where he couldn't touch her, and now she was the one touching him.

She moved her hand away.

His phone trilled with an irritating, old-fashioned telephone ring, and he glanced at her apologetically.

"You're fine," she said curtly. "I'll get a nurse in to finish up with your friend."

She turned on her heel, and Adam stood with his back to her as he talked quietly on the phone.

She closed the door and walked down the hallway to give Weber the lowdown. She checked in with Nurse Pham and signed her forms. The hockey players had been the last of her patients. She was off the clock. Now would be a perfect time to call her mother. She hiked over to the physicians' lounge.

"It's your dad's naptime," May Yin Frobisher said over the phone. "I hate to wake him when it's so hard to get him to sleep."

Helen knew it was. It was why she had chosen to call now instead of later. She squelched down her guilt and became brisk. "Just a quick check-in today. How is his depression?" she asked. "How is the new medication working out for him?"

She and her mother ran through their set list of questions. While they talked, it was easy to forget that this was her mother and that the patient with parkinsonism was her own father.

Satisfied, she was about to hang up, when May Yin said, hesitantly, "Helen, I've been thinking. With your dad's condition being the way it is, we'd like to move to a smaller place. Somewhere without stairs."

"Mum, Dad's doing fine right now. The new medication has been working well. The tremors are under control."

May Yin was silent. She was probably twisting her still-black hair. Her husband and daughter often ganged up to veto her. It never did any good, Helen thought with a sick twist in her stomach. Besides, with her father deteriorating every day, he didn't have a say.

When May Yin spoke again, her voice had become precise and distant. "It would be better for us to move before your father gets worse—"

Helen wanted to open her mouth, but May Yin kept talking, ruthlessly and without inflection. "It is only going to go downhill from here," she said. "I've been asking your brother to look for condos in Vancouver, so that we'll be near him and Gordon, closer to the kinds of medical services that your father needs. Helen, I know it's your childhood home and you love it, but I can't do this anymore. I can't take care of your father by myself. I can't drive hours every week to take him to specialists. I can't pick up after him and cook and keep the house clean—"

"I'll send you money for a housekeeper. And you can hire someone to drive you."

She grimaced as she heard herself. This was exactly the kind of illogic she discouraged in patients and families. And here she was thinking magically, *If I don't go back, my father won't worsen. He'll stay the way I left him. The house will be perfect and welcoming. Everything will be okay.*

She closed her eyes and wished her words back, but her mother, who had a lot to deal with these days, had a short fuse, too. "I know this upsets you, Helen. But I've already made a decision. Besides, if we move, it'll make it easier for you to visit."

May Yin hung up.

Her mother was quietly angry, which Helen was used to. She could hardly blame her mother. Helen had not been to see her parents since summer. She didn't live that far down the coast from them. And added to the fact that she and her father had always been close, she was a neurologist. She could be of use to him.

Except when she couldn't.

She shoved the phone back in her pocket and strode out of the room as if she knew where she was going.

Her father's central nervous system was failing. His brain was shutting down and dying, and here she was with her fancy medical degree, and there was not a thing she could do about it.

–

Adam could not afford to be distracted, least of all by the woman who had just left the room. But her gestures had been so deft, her movements so precise – it was fascinating to watch her, and much more pleasant than the task at hand.

He was dimly aware that the first doctor – Weber, his name was – had come back in and was reassuring him about Serge's health. Of course Serge would be fine. He'd taken worse hits before. But the media attention for this traffic accident was probably going to be ugly, even though the kid was fine. The season had barely started, and the Wolves were already in a losing streak. Worse, this was only the team's second year in operation, but already it was their second year occupying the bottom of the NHL rankings. The town was indifferent to the team unless the players did something stupid. Their billionaire owner was reviled. Hardly anyone showed up to games. Hell, they hadn't even been able to get crowds into the goodwill pancake breakfast they'd held.

And then there was the arena.

The stupid fucking arena.

They needed all the positive publicity they could get. Two team members getting into a car accident with a seventeen-year-old girl would not make for pretty headlines: *Teenager. Accident. Hockey Goons.* Bad optics, someone might say, even though Adam hadn't been drinking or speeding or doing anything reckless. They'd been coming back from a Sunday afternoon benefit for a sports camp when the girl had run a red light and plowed into them. Luckily, the kid was fine, if a little shaken up. Adam felt sorry for her. But now Serge and Adam had a light shining on them, just when it was best to lie low.

Adam already left a message with his and Serge's manager. No doubt the team's GM would be alerted soon enough, as would the media. Adam winced. Some Norwegian player they'd brought in to replace the kid from Duluth had been fired last week. A rookie from Ontario had been dropped two weeks ago. The team was playing badly. Everyone was hanging on to their jobs by a thread. All it took was this kind of thing for someone to find an excuse to can Adam too.

It had taken seven years, but he was now a realist about his career; he wasn't much longer for this gig. If he had been a better player on a better team, he might have looked forward to a career in coaching, or maybe he could become a sportscaster, run a themed bar with decent memorabilia and Guinness on tap. Maybe he could have started a camp. But he wasn't particularly gifted as a player – not like some of the other guys on the Wolves' roster who might have thrived in a different environment. Adam hadn't scored all season and was unlikely to in future. He was the muscle. Muscle was abundant and cheap. It didn't last.

He blew out a frustrated sigh.

Dr. Weber was now offering tips for how to improve his game.

Adam gave him a weak thumbs up. He should be considering his survival strategy. He should be totting up his finances, sweeping the supermarket for dented cans of soup, and making damn sure he could afford to live over the next few years.

13

But a good part of his mind was preoccupied with Helen Frobisher, neurologist.

She was pretty, in a sober, sheltered, breakable way. Brown hair – not chestnut, not auburn. *Brown*. And in a ridiculously tight bun. No makeup. She had delicate ears, a graceful neck, a long thin nose with a slight bump in it, and thin lips, which made her look fastidious and intellectual. Her skin had an olive cast, and yet, it still looked like she spent a lot of time indoors, peering at CT scans, probably, or mixing up mystery formulas. She seemed delicate from far away. But that wasn't what had made him notice her.

After a moment talking to her, looking at her, he'd realized it would be a mistake to think of her as fragile. Her posture was perfect. She spoke crisply, and her eyes were ever alert. It was her hands that really captured him. There was no way she was any sort of weakling, not with such strong, deft hands, which sliced through the air quickly and ruthlessly. The movements of fingers and palm were controlled, but they spoke. *Expressive*, he thought. *Angry*. That was a little surprising. When the gloves came off, he'd met guys on the ice who had less aggression in their fists than Dr. Helen Frobisher.

He wondered what had set her off, and as he'd watched more closely, he grew more conscious of the movement of fine muscles under the arms and shoulders of her white coat. He had learned some things about how people moved, and – well – it was a pleasure to watch her. He had found himself moving closer just to observe. Of course, that had gotten her hackles up, until she pushed him into a chair to make him behave.

And he had liked that last part. A lot.

It was funny. People prodded Adam all the time. Trainers, physios, masseurs, teammates, opponents were always poking him, punching or grabbing his arms, looking at bumps, positioning his limbs and torso. There was always a physician checking his knees, his arms, his hips, a coach eyeing his hands and legs. His body was not his own. But he'd never been examined quite this way by a steely, young woman. When she shone a flashlight in his eyes and started firing questions at him, he felt his skin and guts jump to her commands.

She was compelling. *Formidable.* She was a long line of adjectives fit for an army general. She'd made him focus almost as if she were an opponent, someone facing him on the ice. Her serious, fine-boned face, her sharpness, it was all completely new for him. She made him feel alert, he thought, a little surprised; it hadn't occurred to him that he had been going through the motions lately.

More interesting, she'd clearly reacted to him too. She bristled when he drew near. Sure, her tone seemed even and deliberately mild, her face controlled. But he wondered if she had any idea how vivid her hands were. From the white doctor's coat, her wrists emerged as fragile as a paper crane until they tightened around a pen or sliced through the air to illustrate her thoughts. And then those sinews and bones flexed, and she flashed her penlight right into his eyes like she wished it were a dagger.

He had admired it all way too much.

He had also enjoyed the way she'd needed to stand very close to him, too. One huge brown eye had been practically in his. If she'd tilted her head and he'd bent his and she moved a fraction of an inch sideways, they would have been lip to lip, teeth to teeth, tongue pressed to tongue. Luckily, she pulled back for a minute, and because it was right there, he looked past the curve of her neck and right down her blouse. Sky-blue bra, he noted dizzily. The sight of her skin peeking through fabric and lace would be imprinted in his brain. *Not cool, Magnus*, he had told himself, looking away. Not cool at all.

He blinked himself back to the present, thanked Dr. Weber, then went back to the hallway to call Bobby, his manager, again.

Bobby jabbered worriedly.

Adam said, "No, we weren't drinking at all. Girl plowed through a stoplight and right into us. Serge is out of tomorrow's game."

Bobby wasn't the sharpest manager, but then, Adam wasn't the best player. He and Serge were Bobby's two major clients. He had signed them both years ago, back when their bones were more or less intact and their futures had looked sunny. The rest of Bobby's roster comprised softball players, lesser American marathoners, and a couple of minor league pitchers. He wasn't a shark. Bobby was more of a clownfish, darting in and out and feeding off of the scraps.

Adam being a scrap.

He paced the hospital hallway and tried to concentrate. "Look," he said. "I'm fine. I'm being discharged. Just tell me where they want me to be and what they want me to say, and I'll do it. But Serge is pretty banged up, and he isn't going anywhere."

Within minutes, text instructions began arriving. Adam said good-bye to a sleeping Serge, signed his discharge papers, and looked around for Helen Frobisher.

She strode past him and gave him a short nod. But her eyes looked sad. Never mind. He would never see this woman again.

He took a cab back to the team's offices. He had to admit, the management team was better at crisis than the players were at playing. They'd had more practice. He changed his shirt and went up to the press center. A few people briefed him, but he knew the drill: Say as little as possible, look blank and bland. He would sit beside Coach and answer questions monosyllabically, with long pauses in between words. There was no need to talk about Serge's condition. After less than an hour, they threw the doors open to face the bloggers and writers and sportscasters. After a moment of silence, the management team's faces fell.

Not one reporter had bothered to come.

Chapter Two

"Oh dear God," said Helen, shuddering as the players slammed into the boards again, "I've counted at least four bloody noses, four lacerations to the scalp, and three potential concussions."

Helen and her friends and practice partners, Sarah and Petra, were watching the Wolves get pounded by the Los Angeles Kings. Apparently, this happened on a regular basis. No one else in the bar was paying attention to the game.

"You're supposed to be keeping track of the number of goals and assists, not the number of traumatic head injuries," Petra said, rolling her gray eyes.

"Look at the way that guy is shaking himself. He's dizzy, trying to clear the impact, but he's still skating," Helen said.

She covered her eyes, then peeked through the cracks.

The television in Maloney's Pub was on mute, but Helen could imagine the dull thuds of impact, sharp sounds of skates on ice. She remembered watching her brother at practice. It had been just as horrifying and fascinating then as it was now.

Sarah, Helen, and Petra had met in medical school. They had all matched to Portland hospitals, and even though they had gone into different specialties, they remained friends. They had recently begun a multispecialty practice together in the downtown Pearl District. Petra was an allergist, Sarah an obstetrician/gynecologist, and Helen a neurologist. Keeping up the relationship through medical school and residency had not been easy. Aside from the long hours that they'd kept during their residencies and fellowships, they were competitive and opinionated. It came with the territory. The lack of sleep probably hadn't helped any of their tempers either.

Helen winced again as another pair of players erupted into a brawl. "Damn, that number fifty-two keeps on getting hit with the stick and bounced on the ice. And that's just one game. How many of these do they play every year, anyway? I'd be surprised if he doesn't end up developing chronic traumatic encephalopathy."

"You're really bumming me out, you know?" Sarah said. "Why are we paying attention to this, anyway?"

"It was on when I got here. And I saw a couple of hockey players yesterday, and Dr. Weber called me out for not knowing about the team. It caught my eye," Helen said, perhaps a bit defensively.

Sarah blotted an invisible spot in front of her with a napkin and pushed her straight, dark hair back. "So you're studying up on hockey to suck up to Weber?" she said.

"Maybe I thought the players were cute," Helen said.

Sarah and Petra laughed and laughed.

"What, you mean one of them was wearing a black turtleneck and discussing celestial navigation?" Petra chortled.

"What is that supposed to mean?"

"She means hockey players are so not your type," Sarah said.

"I don't have a type. I find many different men attractive."

"Yeah, but you only date one kind," Petra said.

"The kinds with high foreheads and long noses they can look down," Sarah said.

"Mopey," Petra said.

"Serious."

"The kinds who launch into long monologues about how real books are better than e-books because of the texture and smell of the covers. Guys who moan about *the sensory experience*," Sarah said, rolling her eyes.

"The *sensual* experience," Petra corrected. "Like, I can only love a real book that gives paper cuts to my fingers and *my soul*, not some robo-book that can't love me back."

"The kinds who would spend a lot of time explaining what *feminist* means, to you and me, and to the world."

"That was just one guy, and I only went out with him once – okay, twice," Helen protested. "I was in my twenties. We all went out with that dude."

"I didn't."

"Me neither."

"Maybe it just felt like you went out with him forever."

"Well, you did go out with Dr. Mike for a long time, too, and he was full of himself," Petra said.

Helen winced.

Her first year after finishing her residency had proven particularly bumpy. As if the slog of work and getting her license weren't enough, there had been her father's diagnosis. At the time, she hadn't told anyone. Not her friends, not her boyfriend, Dr. Mike Hardcastle. Then Mike had made noises about getting married. They would have another ideal life, with their careers, and later, kids.

But it wouldn't be perfect, would it? Her father's illness was ugly and getting uglier. It would drain her family. It would take all of her. Helen just *could not*. She couldn't work, be responsible for her father, and be all that Mike wanted her to be.

So. She'd had a one-night stand, broke up with Mike, and confided to Sarah that she'd cheated on him. Upstanding Sarah found her trust in Helen shaken, too – it had nearly ruined their friendship.

But now they were all stumbling along again. And despite the fact that her friends were having fun bringing her down a peg – or several – at least they were still around to do it. Helen knew she liked the chatter better than silence.

Petra and Sarah were still arguing about something or other. Sarah was wrinkling her nose, her brown eyes wide with alarm and laughter.

Helen wished she could join their mirth.

Sometimes, at night, she'd stare at the ceiling wondering exactly how she'd gotten here. She couldn't say that the reckless one-night stand that ended her relationship had been about her dad's condition. Association, after all, was not causation.

Now she admitted that maybe she was not handling her father's illness as well as she'd hoped.

As Petra and Sarah continued to spar, Helen stared moodily at the television screen. Her phone call with her mother yesterday was just another in a series of jolts. If Helen could afford it, she would buy the old house herself. But she had recently invested in the practice, and she had mortgage payments to make on her condo and student loans to pay off. And really, what would she do with a big empty house? She had to preserve her money in case something happened to her father. At least her parents lived in Canada, and the cost of medical care wouldn't deplete their savings. But her father's disease was unpredictable, if inevitable. As May Yin had said, he was only going to deteriorate. All sorts of things could come up: Maybe at some point, her mother would need to hire extra caregivers for her father. Maybe May Yin would need someone to help with housekeeping. Maybe her mother would succumb to the strain and fall ill herself.

Selling the house made sense. If only Helen could admit it out loud.

Helen and May Yin fought a lot more now, but quickly and in hisses. Her brother, wisely, stayed out of it.

She took a swig of her beer and slouched down in her seat.

Her dad had been the last one to accept the diagnosis. He demanded to look at the MRI and CT scans. He saw several neurologists. He even had Helen examine him as if her knowledge of him could reach deep inside and find one misfiring neuron, one small block of misbehaving brain, and tweak it. But they all knew that Harry's doctors could treat his symptoms, but there would be no cure for the disease. Her father's brain was dying, cell by cell. Soon the man who had taught Helen how to listen to a heartbeat, shown her the stars on a clear night, quizzed her about spelling and history and anatomy, delivered her brother, danced with his wife on the porch, soon he would disappear. In a way, he was already gone. The degeneration robbed him of sleep. It made a once vigorous, cheerful, curious man slow and stiff and angry. And the progression of his disease, once they discovered it, had been fast. It was almost as if once Harry had agreed on the diagnosis in his mind, he'd simply opened his fist and let his true self flutter away.

Petra nudged her with her beer bottle. "Hey," her friend said. "You okay there?"

Her friend's gray eyes were sympathetic. And a little worried. That was Petra, always trying to fix things and trying to take on the burdens of the world.

Helen nodded and practiced her deep breathing. She had read a study that found a correlation between meditation and regions of the brain associated with empathy and response to stress. Considering how her thoughts had drifted yesterday with that hockey player, Adam Magnus, she probably needed to improve both her empathy and stress responses.

But she made the mistake of looking at the screen again. "Now they're not even playing, they're just fighting," she yelped, horrified. "They're just going at it, bare knuckled."

"They're wearing helmets," Sarah said, ever contradictory.

Helen winced as the camera closed in on the two players.

"I don't think that's helping," she said, as the dark-haired player's head snapped back. Sweat flew off of the men and onto the Plexiglas behind them. Blood started streaming down the player's nose.

She, Sarah, and Petra leaned in closer to the television set. The men slugged at each other resignedly, with the blond seeming to have the upper hand for a while. Helen watched them slamming into the boards again. And suddenly, she was irrationally angry. Again.

She was getting a little predictable.

"It's kind of mesmerizing," Sarah said, moving a fry to her mouth.

"You're the only one who thinks so," said Petra.

"Not true. Doc Weber's totally with me on this. Right, Helen?"

Petra snorted. "Oh pardon me, $n=2$, where subject one is you and subject two is Weber. Every study population has outliers. In this case, it's the entire population of the Pacific Northwest versus you two. The Wolves madness that afflicts you and Weber is not statistically significant."

"Why are they so unpopular?" asked Helen.

"They're the losingest team in the NHL," Sarah explained. She liked to know everything about anything. "Last year was their first year, so that was at least excusable. But now, they're just an embarrassment. Plus, there's the fact that they want a brand new arena built with city and state funds, even though there are already two perfectly good venues in town for them."

"I heard something about that," Petra said.

"The owner is some billionaire. Totally shady."

Sarah ate another fry while still staring intensely at the game.

On screen, a fist connected with the blond's nose.

"Do they do that in every game?" Helen asked.

"Yeah, I think it's pretty standard," Petra said. She was watching Sarah.

Helen pushed her stool back. "The American Medical Association and the American Academy of Neurology have called for a boxing ban for years. I can't believe they haven't extended it to hockey. At least boxers have gloves and a padded ring. Ice is hard and sticks and skates are sharp."

"Why would they ban it? It's fascinating," Sarah said, chewing distractedly.

"Clearly," Petra said. "Sarah, you do realize that you've put several wedges of deep-fried potato into your pure, kale-fed mouth, right?"

Sarah's eyes widened, and she jerked back, as if hit. On the ice, the players pulled apart.

"A few fries aren't going to kill you, Doc," Petra said.

Sarah opened her mouth to argue, of course, but Helen didn't hear her.

The camera had pulled away to reveal the blond player skating around the rink. It was Adam Magnus.

–

He was too old for this, he thought as he eased into his hotel room bed later that night. He had stitches on his forehead and a yellow and purple bruise on his ribs, and his legs were mottled with black and blue. His roommate and the rest of his teammates – all younger – were out, armed with cash and condoms. The Wolves loved being on the road. They were especially happy when games took them to LA, land of dry heat and hot women. Never mind that they always lost their games – they'd come to expect that part. For Adam's teammates, any place was better than Portland, with its rain, its earnestness, and its lack of fans. As for Portland women, according to his fellow Wolves, they were all bitter shrews who didn't shave their legs – or any other parts. Adam had no idea how any of the Wolves had come upon this knowledge, since none of his women had the bad taste to hang out with these teammates.

Unaccountably, he felt himself thinking of Dr. Helen Frobisher, the woman least likely to show him anything.

God, was he really dreaming about her grooming habits?

He needed a girlfriend.

He also needed to get to sleep so that he'd be able to play the next road games. Unless, of course, he was sent down to the minors yet again.

He recalled the nearly empty press conference the other day and winced. The PR team had geared up for a damage control, but the news outlets that bothered to cover it quoted from the release and then used the accident as a way to rehash the controversy over Yevgeny Molotov's use of tax-exempt government bonds to fund the building of the arena.

Who could blame anyone for finding a mysterious Russian billionaire more interesting than a couple of banged up hockey players? Molotov consorted with models and the mafia. Rumor had it that he had commissioned a bidet from Prada, that he owned a sex island in the South Pacific, and that he had one wife per continent. The citizens of Portland had questions about how exactly he'd gotten the government to fund the new arena. They had questions about why they needed yet another arena to begin with.

And really, frankly, everyone wanted to hear more about the alleged sex island.

Everyone except Adam. He just needed to buy more time to figure out his life.

At least he had a degree, not that he knew what to do with a BA in psych. He had been playing professionally since he was twenty-two. He had socked away a reasonable amount of money but certainly not as much as expected. He'd spent a lot during his lean years in the minors and had poured a lot into his parents' farm. But he didn't know who to talk to about his future. Retirement wasn't something that his goalie friend Serge wanted to contemplate – he was too busy with his own woes – and manager Bobby would freak out if he knew that Adam was planning to jump ship. Adam might have to go back to school. He might have to figure out what he liked to do.

He really didn't have time to think about women.

Adam pulled the sheets up. At least the team sprung for nice hotel rooms, he thought as he fell asleep.

Chapter Three

Concussion.

  Chronic traumatic encephalopathy. CTE.

Helen reached into her bowl of popcorn, stuffed a handful in her mouth, and crunched mindlessly as she reviewed the National Hockey League's concussion protocols, then read through PubMed, loading up on as many articles as she could. None of this was new to her. She'd started considering it as soon as her father's diagnosis had sunk in and she'd begun to suspect his history of boxing. But today, she felt compelled to look at hockey. She hadn't given the sport much thought in recent years. She usually worked with headache and migraine patients, but studying up on her father's condition had given her a renewed interest in degenerative brain diseases like CTE: a series of concussions over a lifetime, like invisible stresses lining a porcelain bowl, would leave the brain fragile until a final tap was all it would take for the delicate structure to shatter.

It used to be called *dementia pugilistica*, boxer's dementia, or punch-drunk syndrome. It started with headaches and minor attention deficits. By the time the disease ran its course, patients had slurred speech, they became angry and aggressive, or jealous and paranoid. They weaved and listed when they walked. Some of the patients were suicidal.

It was linked to parkinsonism, the set of symptoms that her father had.

Boxers, of course, became susceptible to CTE particularly after long years in the ring. So did football players. So did hockey players.

She'd liked the game when she was a kid. Her brother, Stephen, had played because that's what boys did in their town if they wanted to seem "normal." He'd been pretty good, too, but all that pride had turned to horror on the day that Stephen had gotten slashed across the cheek. He'd sunk to the ice, blood pouring out of him, and it was the most terrifying memory of Helen's childhood. A member of Stephen's own team had done that to him. The whole team had been trying to trip up the half-Asian kid that day. Her brother still had the scar.

Helen's parents had withdrawn Stephen from the team after that incident. They'd all worked hard not to think about hockey ever since.

She thought she'd put that awful memory behind her, but now Helen had hockey – or rather, a certain hockey player – on the mind. Every study Helen read, every game she watched, she became more angry. And she had watched a lot of games over the past week.

During her rotations, she had seen patients who battled to put one foot in front of the other, who couldn't remember the names of their spouses or how many children they had. Some patients couldn't read; they couldn't talk. In every way, they became isolated and fearful. That was the worst part of dementia – the loneliness and fear of the patients. Her father had a loving family, but he was alone and afraid, and there was nothing she could do about it. But in rings, fields, and rinks, grown men threw themselves willingly at this kind of brain damage.

Why would anyone make himself into her father? Why would anyone want to be part of that violent culture?

Helen told herself she was detached, that she was just looking into concussion from a clinical point of view. But a corner of her mind knew the truth. Her mind was circling and circling this information because she thought she could do something about it. She couldn't help Harry Frobisher but she could help *someone*.

Her own befuddled mind presented her with a vision of Adam Magnus's sharp eyes.

Ugh. She wished she'd never seen him play. She wished she'd never seen him take off his helmet to reveal his hair dark with sweat, the streak of blood on his forehead. She wished she hadn't seen his shoulders slumped with fatigue, the dullness of his eyes.

It shouldn't matter to her. But it did.

She stood up, flapped her arms, then brought herself down in a deep stretch. She pulled her head up. The coffee table held three bowls and spoons and dregs of milk and crumpled paper napkins. Her couch was a mess of medical journals. On the television, the Kings were playing the Avalanche. She was thirty-two years old; it was a Friday night; and she was in a hoodie, eating popcorn and cereal, reading about brain trauma, and hate-watching hockey.

She was getting weird. She'd end up buried under journals. Her elderly neighbor, Alicia, would probably call the police because of the terrible smell coming from the condo.

She would go out and see her friends, but her breaks hadn't coincided with Petra's, and as an OB/GYN, Sarah's hours were crazy.

Helen decided she'd check in at Stream, the bar that belonged to Petra's boyfriend, Ian. At the very least, she'd find someone there to talk to. Plus, Stream didn't have a television (except during World Cup) because it was classy and snooty. She loved to bug Ian about installing one and observe how far back he could roll his eyes. But tonight, the last thing she needed was to think about hockey.

An hour later, she'd showered away the grime of brooding and bad snacks, waved to her neighbor Alicia who was peering from her windows, and driven into the Pearl District to park her car a few blocks away from her friend's bar.

It had rained earlier in the day, and fog still hovered over the street. But despite the fact that it was November, it wasn't too cold out. She double-wrapped her scarf around her neck and stepped out into the night, strolling slowly along the sidewalks, pausing to peer in the windows of a bookstore or stare at the red shutters of a burned-out building. She loved living here. The Okanagan Valley was her childhood, but it had changed, and now those memories were overlaid with the pain of her father's condition. Here, where she had finally landed, after thin years of classes and study and frantic work, she felt like she was among her people. She could sense the mountains in the distance, silent and impassive. She could breathe.

She stopped for a minute to enjoy the evening and stepped back to let an amorous couple pass.

Their progress was slow. She wondered briefly if she could find funding for a study about French kissing and psychomotor retardation. In fact, she could probably whip up the grant proposal while she was waiting for them, if they continued at this rate.

But as they ambled by, wrapped in each other, another giant pedestrian started along the street behind them. Helen stilled. She recognized that outline, that fuzz of blond hair shining under the streetlights. She found herself in front of the living reminder of her obsession and worry and all that she had been doing in the last week: Adam Magnus.

God, he was tall. Taller than she remembered.

He moved much more gracefully off of his skates. Maybe it was because his back was straight and not crouched over a hockey stick, and maybe it was because he wasn't attired in a sloppy jersey, but with a woolly scarf, jeans, and a tailored tweed blazer.

She had a weakness for tweed.

He was going to look down and catch her staring at any moment now. That really wouldn't do.

Fight or flight, her brain said.

She took a deep breath and felt her leg muscles tense, and she stepped right in front of Adam Magnus on the dark Portland street.

35

"You!" she said, poking him in the chest with her finger. "You were playing the day after you got out from the hospital after a car accident. You let Serge Beaufort play the next goddamn game after that! He had a concussion."

If she was going to feel something for him, she preferred it to be fury.

Adam Magnus looked confused as he gazed down at Helen. Then his face seemed to brighten.

The big lunk.

"The team doctors okayed him to fly in to LA. They said he could lace up," Adam Magnus said slowly. "It's not actually my decision."

There might have been the hint of laughter in his voice.

Maybe flight would have been a better choice, Helen realized. She had not expected him to give her a measured and reasonable explanation.

Adam blinked and gave her a quiet, slow smile. "How's it going, Dr. Helen Frobisher?"

Helen swallowed.

She was ready to fight with him. After all, he was a brawler, wasn't he? But she was the one who was furious and irrational and, for some odd reason, frightened for him, which only fueled her anger more. He wasn't her patient, and he hadn't been seriously hurt. If she was going to worry over anyone, she really ought to have been more worried about Serge Beaufort. His condition had been more serious and easily exacerbated. Clearly, the team doctors were in the pockets of the owners, or managers, or whatever power structure they had in hockey.

Still, Adam Magnus was here, right in front of her, and he'd been the one whom she had been really watching on her screen for the last few days. Sure, she dutifully viewed other games from other teams, staring at the screen through the tunnel created by her hoodie, like a mad solitary bomber. She was researching. But for some reason, Adam Magnus was the man who drew her. She had learned to pick out his number on the jersey. She knew the shape of his broad back, the tilt of his body as it skated across the ice. And now, apparently, she felt like she had a right to tell him how to run his life.

He was still smiling, still watching her as her anger sputtered out. When she stared at her television, it was easy to convince herself that he was someone brutal and callous. Someone who lived by his fists.

But his smile. It changed him.

She suddenly realized where she was and who she was. She removed her finger from his chest. "Mr. Magnus," she said, backing away.

"It's Adam."

"Right."

She stepped back even more, aware that she was not exhibiting healthy human behavior. What kind of person – what kind of doctor – launched herself at people on the street and screamed at them to take better care of themselves?

"I'm sorry," she said, stiffly. "I shouldn't have poked you. Or yelled."

Adam Magnus looked amused. "You wouldn't be the first," he said.

She peered at him. "You have a new laceration on your forehead," she said.

He grimaced. "Not pretty, is it? Well, because you were apparently watching the games, you'll know that I got clobbered pretty hard in LA." He paused. "You seem to know more about the team now."

He sounded pleased.

"I studied up," said Helen. "Apparently, I embarrassed myself the other day."

And tonight, she thought.

Adam's face twisted into a grimace. "Well, not a lot of people in Portland really seem into hockey," he said. "We're working on it," he added.

He seemed far from the arrogant, blustering jock that she expected him to be. Of course, he'd never acted cocky, not even in the hospital. Helen had no idea why she thought that would be his personality.

"Well," she said, "I don't care about how well your team does. I'm more concerned about the potential for injury."

Inside, she winced. Could she sound *more* priggish and insulting? She stepped back and waved – a signal that she was going to leave. But he moved close to her again. He seemed to want to go with her. "Why don't I walk you wherever you're headed?" he said. "It's late."

"This is a safe neighborhood. I don't want to put you out," she muttered.

She shot a sideways glance at him. He shrugged, an easy, graceful roll of those shoulders that somehow left

Helen a bit breathless. "That's a nice scarf. Very... er... jazzy."

"Jazzy. That's good, right?" He added, "I've got a night off. I needed to think, so I decided to walk around. I live around here." Almost to himself, he added, "And I'm going to miss it when I'm gone."

She resolutely did not ask him what he meant.

They walked slowly toward Stream, not saying much, both seemingly preoccupied. But most of Helen's thoughts had been about him for days. She found it hard to concentrate with this man beside her. She tried not to study him, but live and in the flesh, he was so much person. It was difficult not to stare at his hands, for instance, his wide palms and flat knuckles, which had smashed into jaws and guts countless times, but which, swinging by his sides, looked like they would do well on a piano, spanning octaves and tenths or moving nimbly over arpeggios. Abruptly, her brain devised a test of his fine motor skills, using his fingers and her skin, and she swallowed and swung her gaze away. It was easier to watch him when he was boxed in by television. On television, he was brutal. In person, he was dangerous.

Where had that thought come from?

Nevertheless, she was glad when they reached the safety of the bar. With other people around, she wouldn't fixate on him.

Stream was lively and warm. The copper fixtures gleamed brightly under the lights of hurricane lamps. Laughter and chatter rose and ebbed. She and Adam stood in the doorway for a minute, their eyes still needing time to adjust. He had pressed his hand on the small of her back, the lightest touch of fingers. And he turned his head and leaned into her so delicately, as if he wanted to shelter her under the protective curve of his body, as if he were asking a question.

She wanted to say yes.

The evening seemed to have turned into something entirely different from the one she had planned.

Helen took in a breath.

She peered around the bar to see if Petra or Sarah was there, or even the manager, Lilah. But although she knew and nodded at most of the servers, she didn't see her friends.

"Let's get that booth," Adam said in her ear, giving her another light press of his fingers. She felt her body thrill under his hand.

He helped her take her jacket off and hung it up for her. He waited for her to sit down, then slid in next to her.

She cleared her throat. "You have good manners," she said.

"Minnesota farm boy," he said. "We're polite, stoic, and surprisingly good singers."

"You were a choirboy?"

"There was a lot of Handel in my youth."

"I'll bet you looked angelic, with your blond hair and bright eyes."

"*Sing forth, seraphim and cherubim*, as they say. Or at least that's what Handel says."

40

She had a sudden vision of him as a Renaissance angel, except not one of those insipid halo wearers, but glorious and powerful, the muscles of his naked back straining as he wrestled with a mortal.

Luckily, the server, Juliet, came by and took their drink orders and handed them menus.

He didn't look at his menu. "What's good here?" he asked Helen.

"The hush puppies are really good. They change the food pretty frequently."

"Come here often?"

"A friend owns it. A lot of the food comes from surrounding farms or fisheries. The wine and beer are all from Oregon, too."

She was glad to be talking about something innocuous and impersonal, especially because of the way he was glancing at her. Still, the whole thing seemed to be escalating between them almost without provocation. During the small talk, there were quick glances, a brush of her thigh against his. Maybe later, a touch of hands, lips, tongues.

Still later – she could almost smell its heady scent – sex.

She was going to put that on the table, and he looked like he would take the offer. Now that she'd defined her desire in her mind, she felt a little more in control of the situation. She could tell herself that he'd somehow managed to maneuver her into this, that he'd dazzled her somehow, that he'd worked some sort of athletic jock magic on her: dazzled her with his thigh muscles and forearms and the diamond cut of his cheekbones. He had.

And yet, she had not objected, and would not, although she had many opportunities. She had not ordered him to go home when they reached the bar or shaken off his hand when he put it on her back. She had not refused his help with her coat or told him not to sit down. She was flirting. She let her eyes roam openly over his lips, shoulders, and chest. In fact, now that they were sitting down next to each other, she wished that he'd touch her.

The server came back with wine and a plate of warm, spicy smelling potatoes. "*Patatas bravas*," Juliet said. She indicated a bespectacled man behind the bar. "Ian sent it over. He says he'll come by later."

They chorused their thank-yous, gave their orders, and Adam waited for her to take a piece. She set it on her plate and looked up. He was staring at her. They were staring at each other. Still looking at him, she took a small sip of wine. He followed suit.

This was *so* a date.

No, it wasn't, she reminded herself. If anything, he was trying to get lucky and so was she. They had nothing in common except a dark vein of attraction.

It was enough.

Luckily, or unluckily, Ian came up and dropped a kiss on the top of her head.

"Hey Ian, don't you have a manager who covers this place?" Helen said brightly. "And where's Petra?"

"Lilah's out sick, so I'm covering tonight. Petra said she'd be in later, but she's trying to learn about her Indian heritage by making paneer."

"And you left her alone?"

"I kept offering suggestions. The cat's less opinionated, apparently. She's gotten pretty good at a lot of dishes, but making cheese is a whole other level."

She introduced the men and allowed Ian to relax Adam with chatter. Adam was good-natured, and Ian affably extracted all relevant information. Ian was probably memorizing Adam's details for a full report to Petra – how tall he was, what his voice sounded like, what he ate, what he drank, how he looked at Helen. And Adam *was* looking at her. He chatted easily with Ian, but she felt his eyes flit over her profile, her hair, her forest green sweater. Ian noticed Adam's gaze, too, and he seemed amused.

Finally, Ian clapped Adam on the back and promised them some new dishes that the chef was trying out. Ian gave Helen a wry grin and dove back into the room.

A plate of salmon arrived, followed by some sort of root vegetable hash. There was also a plate of bruschetta with a green spread on it and a dish of halibut fritters. Helen wasn't hungry. Although she was interested in watching Adam Magnus as he peered at the food. He looked almost like a little boy as he took a tentative bite of the salmon and chewed thoughtfully. "That's good," he rumbled approvingly. "Although, I could probably eat three or four plates of this."

"They are small. I don't think it's against the rules to order more."

He grinned, then looked over at her. "Aren't you having any?"

"I ate a lot of popcorn at home," she said. "And cereal. Maybe there were some Pop-Tarts."

"I didn't see you as a Pop-Tart kind of girl."

"What does that mean? You don't find me sweet and delicious?"

"I figured you for something more complicated and harder to pronounce."

"Something hard to get my mouth around?"

She heard his light intake of breath even as he narrowed his eyes at her heavy-handed innuendo. When he spoke again, his voice was even.

"I thought of you," he said, pausing very deliberately, "as a more complicated flavor."

He bit into the bruschetta almost delicately, showing her his white teeth. Then he dabbed carefully at the corners of his mouth with a napkin.

His eyes gleamed.

Helen laughed, but her stomach felt tight and fluttery. She took a sip of wine. "This from a man who accessorizes with scarves."

"It's warm, not just jazzy."

"You're never going to let me live that word down."

He ignored her. "To sum up, I'm a sophisticated gentleman with urbane and practical tastes and you're a Pop-Tart."

Helen sat back and marveled. "You know, the problem with you is that you're smarter than I'd like you to be."

"I think that might be your problem, not mine."

She looked at her glass. She was not getting tipsy. Still, she felt the warm pulses of excitement spreading across her body. She was going to do something reckless tonight. She deserved it.

As if in response, he touched his knee against hers and didn't withdraw it this time. She put her hand on his elbow. His bicep looked temptingly hard. It tightened as she traced it with her index finger.

He watched the progress of her hand.

"How did you know that you wanted to be a doctor?" he asked.

Hmm. Not the question she'd been expecting. She withdrew her hand.

"Well, I didn't, at first. I trained for years and years to become a dancer. Ballet."

"Oh, that explains it," Adam said.

"Explains what?"

"It explains how you move. You talk with your body a lot. Your movement has a lot of power. When your arm waves, your head sometimes follows, but your torso remains absolutely controlled."

She cocked her head. "Most people tell me I'm graceful when they hear I danced."

"You're not really – or at least that's not the first thing that comes to mind. Anyway, I interrupted you. You wanted to be a ballerina."

She grabbed a piece of bruschetta and took a thoughtful bite.

"Well, no, I don't know that I wanted to be a dancer," she said. "But I was reasonably good at it, and I won a spot at the San Francisco Ballet's school—"

"That sounds more than reasonably good."

"Just reasonably good. Believe me, there's always someone better. But at the time, I didn't think about it much or even really understand what I was doing until I was eighteen."

"What happened when you were eighteen?"

"When I was eighteen, I got into an accident. I was supposed to – well, instead I ended up in the hospital. In retrospect, it was the best thing to ever happen to me. I mean, in the dance movies, I guess I'm the girl who just doesn't make it, like the great tragic figure whose failure makes the main dancer take a good hard look at who she has become. But it wasn't a tragedy, especially by that time. I realize now that I wasn't happy. I just didn't know what else I could do until the accident forced me to think about my future another way."

He was listening to her like no one else had ever listened before. And she was blabbing things to him that she hadn't really shared with anyone else. For a big, active man, he could be surprisingly still.

"How did you become a hockey player?" she asked.

He frowned and pushed some vegetables around his plate. Did he think of them as pucks? "I played when I was a kid. In fact, it sounds a lot like your life. I wasn't that great. But I never got in the accident, and I just kept on, through college. I was drafted after I finished my degree, and now here I am, still doing the same things. And maybe now taking a good hard look at what I've become."

"Except you were probably a lot more talented than I was."

46

"Just reasonably good."

She laughed, and that made him smile that half smile that set her skin prickling again.

"So why doctoring?" he asked.

"I didn't love ballet, but I did love what the body could do, how the body healed itself, how people could help it along. Plus, my dad was a doctor. Not a neurologist. He was a small-town general practitioner. He saw everyone from age zero to one hundred and did everything from extracting dimes from noses, to emergency deliveries."

"He's passed away?"

Her lips tightened. "No."

She looked down, aware of the concern that touched his face. She took a few minutes to gather herself, then flicked her eyes up again. She held his steady gaze. "Maybe we should get out of here," she said.

Chapter Four

If someone had told Adam that at the end of the night, he would come home with Helen Frobisher, he would have laughed. But here she was, in her slim jeans and that soft green sweater that made him want to rub his cheeks against her, catch his stubble on the smooth knit. He let his fingers brush it as he helped her with her jacket.

Now, she stood in front of his shelves, holding a high-ball glass full of water and tilting her head to scrutinize his pictures, his houseplants, his old Black Sabbath CDs, and a small collection of paperbacks. Most of his music and books were digital now, and he had an irrational wish to open his electronic devices up for her approval. But then, there wasn't more to this, was there?

Everything about her made him want to touch. She wanted it, too, it seemed. On the way back, there had been small bumps of thigh and knee, heavily clothed elbow against elbow, a hand splayed on a back, a brush of the shoulder. She had been so close to him at one point that her chin gilded the sleeve of his upper arm. Almost a kiss. Her long, straight hair gave off the luster of polished wood, but he knew when he slipped his fingers in it, it would be a living thing, whispering seductively on his skin. But his superstitions held him back. He didn't want her to disappear like a dream as soon as she was in his arms.

His pulse was thrumming wildly. Just having her in his apartment, running her fingers over his books, leaning on his couch, her lips on the rim of a glass that he drank from, it was making him wild. Because, after all, he had imagined her here on his furniture, settled against the railing of his terrace, or in his bed, and some of it was coming true already. Sharp, elegant Helen Frobisher.

He was going to be cool about this. He was very cool.

Then she turned and asked to see his bedroom.

He was not going to swallow his tongue.

It wasn't a huge or lavish apartment, but he had glorious floor-to-ceiling windows, and, on clear days, a view of Mount Hood, which he loved. It was probably the nicest place he'd ever lived in. He had bought it in a fit of optimism when he first signed with Portland. He thought the team would go places. It seemed a long time ago. He would probably have to give the space up if he went back to school. Not that he was sure that was where he was headed.

He looked around the place to see what she saw. It was clean, at least. His mother had insisted that all her children be neat, and learn to wash their clothes, and dust and put things away. Not that he had a lot of things. He had big, boxy furniture, chosen to suit his large frame, and a huge television, which he considered a professional expense.

He let her precede him through the hallway. She peered in the bathroom. It seemed to meet with her approval. She looked at the guest room, which he used as an office. The desk was piled with college pamphlets and a copy of *What Color is Your Parachute?* But she didn't seem to pay much attention to that either. At least, she didn't comment on it.

Then she stepped into the last doorway.

She frowned.

"Those are maple leafs," she said, heading for the picture that was conveniently located right above his bed. "Stylized *Canadian* maple leafs."

"Yeah, like in *Slap Shot*."

She looked at him blankly.

"In the movie *Slap Shot*, Paul Newman's a hockey player. He has a Canadian flag over his bed. You've never seen it? It's pretty much the greatest hockey movie ever made."

"This is a crowded genre?"

"Oh fine, Doc, what's the masterwork depicting your profession? *Awakenings*? *Patch Adams*?"

"Ouch. Why do you get to be played by Paul Newman while Robin Williams is me?"

"Are you taking potshots at Robin Williams?"

"No, I'm saying that although he could've done a mean impression of me, he doesn't look anything like a half-Chinese, half-English thirty-two-year-old woman. Not plausible."

"Are you really surprised that Hollywood turned you into a white man at the first opportunity? Besides, they couldn't find anyone pretty enough."

She wrinkled her nose at him and turned back to the maple leaf. "You had your flag Warholized," she said, leaning over the bed for a better angle. Her head was twisted up into a completely uncomfortable position, and her butt stuck out tensely.

All he needed to do was run his hand over her flanks and give her a little push. She'd be sprawling on the sheets, confused, angry, gorgeous.

Art. Clearly, he needed more of it.

"You're very together," she said, coming back to straight posture. "With the handsome, manly furniture, the maple leaf print, the suits and blazers, the jazzy scarf."

"Again with the *jazzy*?"

He took a step toward her.

Her eyes flared. Oh, this was going to be good. But she put her hands between them.

"Rules of the game," she said. "Let's agree on them before we drop the puck, so to speak."

"You know, you don't have to use hockey metaphors. I can understand regular talk just fine, so long as you speak real slowly."

"Does it annoy you when I talk hockey? I'd just like things to be clear before we start the stick handling."

"Shall I call you Mr. Williams, or do you prefer Robin?"

She reached out to give him a little shove, but his hand snapped out and caught her wrist.

They stood looking at the way he held her, his thumb and forefinger circling around her delicate joint, his blunt fingers touching at the ends. Her skin was warm and the power running through her veins and sinews almost electric. She was a strange flower glowing under the lights of his bedroom. He turned her arm so that her wrist faced upward and stroked across the blue veins with his thumb. He could feel her pulse beating fatly, and when he looked up, he saw her eyelids flutter. *She's excited*, he thought. *She's as excited as I am.*

"Rules of the game," she repeated coolly. "This is a one-time thing. We are not involved emotionally. I will leave by morning. If you want me to exit at any time earlier, you will say so instead of being surly or distant in order to drive me away. When I leave, I will extend you the same courtesy."

"Your breath is coming faster."

"That's because I know that we're going to fuck each other's brains out," she said evenly.

Well, that statement certainly contained its own inevitability. He was hard before the sound died on her prim little lips.

She had poise and steel. He felt evenly matched. If a small part of his brain niggled at him that they shouldn't do this and he didn't much like this game or these rules, he ignored it. After all, he was still playing another sport that he didn't particularly like anymore, and it was the best he could expect.

"Okay," he said, letting go of her wrist, "I agree to the terms. Take off your clothes. Please."

He quirked a smile.

"Such good manners, farmer boy," she murmured, reaching for the hem of her sweater.

He shook his head. "Jeans first," he said. "Please."

He planned to touch the sweater on her before she took it off.

She slipped off her shoes and socks and undid the top button and worked the jeans down her hips. Her underwear came down a little way, revealing a strip of brown hair between her legs.

Adam swallowed hard and took a small step toward her. There wasn't room for many more steps.

She lifted one long leg out of the pants, and a lean blade of muscle flexed on the outside of her thigh. His eyes traveled down to the firm calf, down the ankle to her tortured dancer's foot.

God, she was beautiful.

She pulled down the other leg quickly and tossed the jeans on a chair.

"What next?" she asked.

They were both trying to act controlled, both trying to act faintly amused, as if this happened all the time.

"The boy shorts," he said.

If he spoke too much, his voice would betray him.

"I'm impressed that you know the correct lingerie terminology," she said, turning around.

She peeped over her shoulder, then slung her fingers into her underwear.

So did he.

He tugged the band down and stopped just at the curve of her firm butt. "You know," he murmured in her ear, "with an ass like this, you should never, ever wear pants."

He could hear the catch in her breath. Good. But she had her revenge as she bent over, taking far more time than she needed to slide the lace and silk down the rest of her legs.

His jeans were much too confining. He started on his buttons and had his underwear, pants, socks, and shoes off before she could finish her slow slide back up.

She uncurled her back, vertebra by vertebra. He could practically see each joint ticking smoothly into place. He slid his hands over the lush softness of that sweater, then beneath it to her warm skin while she unhooked her bra. He traced the underside of her breasts, watching her watching his hands as he rounded up to her nipples and brushed them with his thumbs. She gasped and pushed herself into his hands, causing her bottom to come up and slide against his thighs.

He pulled her sweater off, deciding that he didn't have the patience anymore to wait. He took off his shirt and tossed it behind him somewhere, and when her back finally touched him, she rubbed her shoulder blades into his chest hair and sighed. That sound, and the feeling of her budded nipples under his thumb and fingers, the smoothness of her back as she undulated against his cock, that was what did him in.

As he moved her toward the bed, she turned and breathed deeply. "You smell like Icy Hot," she said, her head in his chest.

"I'm sorry," he said. "I…"

But she smiled up at him, almost shyly, and he let the small moment bloom around him. When had he ever felt like this before? Never. Yes, he was excited and eager. But he felt much more, and he wanted to examine it. But it was over too soon. Her eyes turned mischievous, then steely. She gave a too-gentle stroke from the base of his prick to the tip. He let out a strangled sound and slid his fingers down her ass and sunk his fingers in. She rubbed her greedy body against him hard, harder. "Why aren't you inside me?" she hissed.

He barely had the strength to leave her to go to the bedside table and take a condom out. By then, she was bent over the bed, legs spread, waiting for him, moaning for him. He rolled the condom on quickly and turned her around. "We haven't even kissed," he said.

"Just shut up and screw me," she said, spreading herself on the bed.

She was really quite flexible.

But that wasn't going to do. He brought her up so that she was sitting against the headboard, and kneeled between her legs. He sat her on his thighs, cupped her ass, and brought her up. And as he kissed her, he finally, finally drove into her, bringing himself up on his knees, bringing her on her heels, her rump against the headboard, feeling the muscles in her ass squeeze and release and squeeze and release in rhythm with him as he drove into her strong little body.

He was dimly aware of her hands, sliding across his sweat-slicked back, urging him on. Her hair was flying wildly forward and back, her tongue and teeth working against his frantically.

She pulled her mouth away from his and moaned. Her head rolled down like a rag doll's and then sprang up again fiercely. She was on her toes, he thought dazedly. He just about lost it right there. Her legs must have been trembling, she should have been tired, but her eyes were level with his and she looked right into him, challenging him, never giving him any quarter. *Let's see what else you can throw at me*, she seemed to say.

She was going to kill him.

He took a deep breath and pulled her into him to sit. They were still for a moment, looking at each other, assessing. Then she tapped him on the shoulder. "On your back," she said, running her hands through her hair. She lifted herself to help him. He felt her every small movement on his cock and it nearly caused him to yowl. Finally, excruciatingly, he managed to shift slowly down and backward. There still wasn't enough room for him to stretch out his legs. She shook her head and removed herself from him, so that he could resettle himself.

"Satisfied?" he grumbled.

"We're getting to that part," she said sweetly.

He gritted his teeth as she settled herself onto him again. Still, she didn't start the rhythm again.

She ran a finger down his chest and back up to his lips. "I could do with some kissing, now," she said, managing to sound almost normal. Only the squeeze of her pelvic muscles gave her away.

"I could do with some fucking, now," he said, tightly.

She threw her head back and laughed, and he wondered how he'd been able to live without that sound for the last twenty-nine years. But her movement was enough to launch her into rhythm again. And he pulled her head down again with one hand, and kissed her wildly, and pushed his palm against her with the other hand, until she let herself go, with a cry, and he let himself crash around her until there was no more he could do.

–

She wasn't sneaking out, per se, but their deal had been that they should be courteous and mature. It would have been infinitely more rude if she woke him. It would be even ruder if she refused to leave his bed – and that's just what she'd been tempted to do.

Still, she felt guilty. After all, it was hardly adult of her to be leaving a note in eyeliner – the letters huge and smudged – but he had been a lot more than she expected. Oh sure, there was the blind pleasure from the man, the sort of wild fuck that involved sensitized nerve endings and bruises in odd places the next morning. But he had been much too engaging in other ways.

Helen rolled her eyes at herself.

She told herself she was reading too much into him. In the light that filtered into the bedroom, Adam was still lethal looking, a gleaming, powerful man. The tendons of his neck and the firm parcels of muscle across his chest and abdomen were gilded with light blond hair, and they seemed poised to ripple at the slightest sound. She pulled the sheet over him, trying not to lick his honey-gold skin. He was just a man, a man with the faint remnants of a farmer tan, golden freckles over his nose and cheeks.

He was beautiful and human, and she didn't want to admit that to herself.

At least she had the excuse of morning rounds to propel her out of his apartment. Although, had he awakened, she would have stayed and gone to work in her grubby clothing. Good thing he was asleep, then. Good thing those light eyes couldn't read her. She couldn't afford to drift into something now. *Especially with him*, she thought, even though she wasn't sure why he warranted extra caution.

She pursed her lips and strode out into the early morning.

A hit of morning air would make her sensible.

He didn't know anything about her. Well, except for what made her thrash like a woman possessed. Then again, he was an athlete. Lucky women all over the country, all over Canada – in every city that had a hockey franchise – had probably experienced that look and that knowledge of anatomy. And, after all, human physiology was fairly predictable. She had managed to make him groan and yell and strain every muscle of his beautiful body, just as he had hers.

The morning air wasn't doing her any good. She unzipped her jacket and closed her eyes.

When she opened them again, her message alert pinged and she panicked for a moment, wondering if it was Adam. But as she fumbled in her bag, she reminded herself that he didn't even have her number.

It was from Petra. *How was his stick handling?*

She shook her head and punched in Petra's number. "How did you do that? Did you make Ian slap a listening device on my shoulder? Do you and Ian have some sort of ESP connection that lets you see the world through his eyes and solve crime? Because it explains so much about you two."

"I didn't know for sure," Petra said. "But Ian told me that he saw a certain something between you two."

"A certain something? Those were his exact words?"

"I don't remember exactly what he said. Maybe something about chemistry, biology, physics," Petra said. "Clearly it enabled me to make an educated guess. Plus, this was Adam Magnus, that hockey player guy, right? The one you were watching so closely on the screen the other evening? Did you *score*?"

Helen looked around for her car. And for Petra. She still wasn't convinced that her friend wasn't following her.

"You know, we can use something other than hockey metaphors," Helen said.

The phrase made her blush furiously as she remembered Adam telling her the same thing just before they began shedding their clothes.

"Good, because I don't know many more," Petra said. "So… it's been a while since the last time, hasn't it?"

There was a slight hesitation in her friend's voice. Probably because the last time had been when Helen cheated on Mike. She'd managed to put that completely out of her mind last night. She was not sure if this was a good thing or a bad thing.

"Helen, all teasing aside, are you okay? I just want to make sure."

"I'm fine. I'm just... muddled. It's been a strange week for me, and then last night happened, so I didn't get much sleep."

Helen looked around desperately and let out a breath. Where was her damn car? She was sure she had parked it on NW 9th.

"Are you going to see him again?"

"No."

"Why not?"

"We agreed it was a one-time thing. It just doesn't make any sense. We come from different worlds."

"Well, you and your ex-boyfriend came from the same background. Look how that turned out."

"Petey," Helen snapped, "I know there's a long tradition of girlfriends talking about the morning after, but I'm pretty sure that the postmortem isn't supposed to leave *me* feeling dead inside."

She found her car.

"I'll leave it alone, then," said Petra.

"Do that."

A pause.

"But just know that I know that you've got a lot going on. And I'm always here for you."

Helen slid into her car and put her head on the steering wheel. "Yes, I know," she whispered.

She didn't have time for self-recrimination or self-congratulation. She drove home and showered, biked to the hospital, and did rounds. Her work was absorbing, and she didn't have time – need time – to process her night with Adam Magnus. When she returned from her shift, she looked at the wreckage of her living room. She picked up the cereal bowls, pried the spoons out of them, and washed them in the sink. She threw out the popcorn scraps, stacked textbooks and journals, and ferried them to the shelves of her never-used study. She vacuumed under the couch cushions and dusted the window sills. She wiped down her coffee table. For good measure, she watered her already-dead plants.

The cheating had been a one-time thing, too, or so she hoped. She had broken up with Mike the next day. Well, she had tried. Dr. Mike, being Dr. Mike, had refused to accept the tepid reasons she'd given him in an attempt to spare his feelings. He'd tried to argue for days that they were still together. He even went and bought tickets for both of them for the ballet and told her to make time in her schedule for it.

As for the guy she slept with, she hadn't felt the urge to carry on with him. He had been a warm body. She had used him, yes, and he had used her. If anything, afterward, she felt numb.

She had made her terms clear, just as she had with Adam Magnus. In fact, the Adam Magnus thing was exactly the same, she decided. She felt absolutely no urge to ever see him again. None.

Okay, so they had been very good together.

That didn't necessarily mean anything.

Despite her efforts, her condo looked neglected. She had never bothered to change the bland office carpeting, the beige walls, or the cheap fixtures. It was clear that the place had been furnished in the spirit of absentmindedness. She had brick and board shelves, and the battered Mission-style couch was a discard from her parents' house. She remembered after her father's car accident, she'd rushed up to see him and he'd protested that he was fine. He seemed fine, but he'd wanted her to take the old piano back to Portland with her, even though she didn't play and there wasn't room for the instrument in her old Honda. He had been upset with her, insisting that she bring it with her, trying to push it out of the living room with his shoulder. He hadn't even unplugged the lamp or removed the metronome. At first she laughed, thinking he was joking. But he had begun to shake. At the time, she had just been preoccupied with calming him down. She should have noticed, at that point, how quick to anger he was, how much his hands trembled, how shadowed his eyes were. How, for a few moments, it was as if he was paralyzed. Had symptoms been there for her to read? Or was her guilt making her misremember?

And what good would it have done to find out earlier?

She hadn't bothered furnishing the place with much else. Even her bedroom was sad and neglected. A part of her had thought that she would be moving in with Dr. Mike. Although, now that she considered it, she wondered why she had bothered to buy a condominium if that had been her plan.

It seemed she was very good at ignoring the obvious.

Adam Magnus had art. Okay, so it was kitschy tribute art to a hockey movie, but still, it looked good in his apartment. He had books. He didn't seem to need her approval even though he had it. He was an adult. He wore scarves.

All the more reason to avoid the man.

She resisted the urge to turn on the television. She could not get sucked into the black hole of Wolves hockey or spend the evening ogling Adam's cheekbones. She should look into more clinical trials. She'd research medication combinations and attempt to find a cure for parkinsonism using the power of her brain, her tablet, and Google.

She decided to make popcorn when the phone rang. She tackled it.

"Helen, you have to come up," May Yin Frobisher said. "It's your father."

Chapter Five

The results of the career aptitude test Adam had taken online said that he should be a writer or a mechanical engineer. Not what he'd call helpful, he thought, settling back on the slightly plastic pillows of another hotel room in another city. They deflated slowly under him as he stared at his iPad.

Writer of what? Advice? Technical manuals? The last thing he'd actually sat down to write was an essay on cognitive behavioral therapy for a class he'd taken, oh, seven years ago in college. And how could he be a mechanical engineer if it had taken him more than fifteen minutes to figure out how to use the shower in this hotel room?

He had been on the road for months, it seemed, although it was probably only a day or two. He was paying little attention to his teammates and had no idea where they all were. Colorado? Arizona? Utah? Did Utah even have an NHL team?

The traveling used to be the easiest part. For a Minnesota farm boy, those days on the road had been heady stuff. Getting on a plane! A different city every week! He was surprised he hadn't strolled through every town with a straw hat and a piece of hay clamped in his jaw.

The novelty wore off sometime around the third year, though, just as his career began to tank. It was too bad. He had gotten good at travel. He'd started wearing suits because they were practical – almost a uniform. He didn't have to think too much about what went with what: The jacket always matched the pants. Plus, someone else cleaned them. But looking across the room at his garment bag hanging in the open closet, the constant grind of packing and unpacking, sealing aftershave and toothpaste in little Ziploc bags, trying to sleep at strange times, thumps from adjoining rooms, the squeals of the mattress… he felt the weariness down in the marrow. Playing hockey was physically bruising, but the long game of planes and travel and time zones was what would really kill him. The one good thing about being on the road was that it gave him an excuse to read *Harry Potter*, again.

He made an appointment with a career counselor for when he got back to Portland. No sense in putting the decisions off any longer. The team had been slowly but steadily extending its losing streak. The Finnish center, Pekka Aro, had been replaced yesterday or the day before by a grunting Swede whose name Adam couldn't remember. Somewhere along the line, they'd lost another right wing, an assistant coach, and their entire PR team. At least Adam was underpaid enough to escape the gun. For now.

Serge, his roommate for the road trip, lumbered out of the bathroom, smoothing his hair. Adam rose, wincing at the sore tendons in his knee, and found some ice.

"You never come out anymore," Serge said.

"I haven't come out all year," Adam said, shrugging.

Serge sat down heavily in one of the chrome and leather chairs and looked around the room.

"How are you going to meet a nice girl if you sit in our hotel room, watching the porn?" he asked, rolling the final r in his light French Canadian accent.

He did it on purpose. Adam could never decide whether Serge sounded classy or creepy. A little of both, probably.

"How am I ever going to find a nice girl if I go out with you?" Adam asked. Most women liked Serge. He was tall enough, but not intimidatingly so, and those French Canadian vowels and consonants made him seem European.

Adam dropped into a chair opposite and settled the ice pack on his knee.

Serge took a sip and put his feet on the coffee table. "Tell me the truth, Adam, why have you been hiding?"

Adam rubbed his face. Serge wouldn't blab to Bobby, but he wasn't sure that the goalie would be sympathetic. But Serge knew him well. He probably already sensed that Adam was on the brink of some kind of major decision. Serge must have been thinking about it himself. He had been in the game as long as Adam had – longer. He hadn't bothered with college, going straight to the draft when he was eighteen. Then again, he hadn't gone down to the minors – yet. Serge was a happy-go-lucky guy.

The only thing that had made Adam happy in recent times was Helen Frobisher, memories of Helen Frobisher, the timbre of her voice, the grip of her hands, the clutch of her bare thighs, the lingering scent of her on his pillows. He hadn't changed his pillowcases. He hoped that the essence of her wouldn't disappear by the time he returned. It was… pretty pathetic. The woman wouldn't ordinarily give a guy like him the time of day. She'd made that clear enough. The night had started more as a curiosity for her, a technical competition, but by the end of the night, he had found out that she pointed her toes when she came.

Those feet. Scarred, tough. Her hands and her feet told him more about her than she did herself. She had endured. Probably worn a smile on her face. She had done something that stretched and pained her body, and she had done it willingly.

Who knows how much better they could be if they had agreed to more than one night? But the echo of her perfume and an ever-worn loop of their encounter, that was all he was going to have of her, he told himself grimly. It was what he had agreed to, and he had taken it dumbly and without thinking, just like he had made every decision in his life before and now.

He really should have stolen her underwear.

Maybe he needed to apply this ice pack to his groin.

"I don't know how much longer this is going to last," Adam finally said. "The team's bad, the press is indifferent, the public's hostile, and I'm not getting better."

"You Minnesota farm boys are all the glass-half-empty kind of people," Serge said. "My theory is that you spent too much time inhaling the tractor fumes and stepping in the cow dung. Makes you guys think you know things about the universe or something. Me, if I blow through all my money, I have a position at my parents' restaurant in Montreal waiting for me. I say, live it up while we're on top."

"We're not on top, Serge. And I'm tired, and I don't have as much saved up as you. And I'm too old for this shit," Adam said, ignoring his friend. He sighed. "I met someone."

"Ah, now the truth comes out."

"This great, interesting, smart, difficult woman who turned me inside out. Someone who I would want to imagine spending my life trying to figure out, except I have no life to spend. I can't even sort myself out, and my future. What makes me think I can go after her or anyone like her?"

"Well, you want her, isn't that enough? Most people don't give it much thought beyond that."

"It wouldn't be enough for her. I wouldn't be enough. Besides, she made it clear that it would be a fling."

"So, you've already slept with her? My friend, if you've shucked the oyster, you can definitely make the stew."

"Jesus, I don't even want to know what the hell that's supposed to mean."

"It means that she agreed to sleep with you. Unless she had a terrible time, it means she will always consider doing it again. She did have a good time, didn't she?"

Adam considered her big brown eyes deep with longing and sorrow, the way she had held back – until she hadn't. He remembered the surrender of her thrashing body, the dark ripple of her final cry.

He shrugged again. "I'm not going to pine for things I can't have."

Except he was.

Serge leaned in. "Maybe you should aim higher. Visualize the results you want."

"That's part of the problem," Adam muttered. Then his eyes widened. "Oh, seriously? You're attempting to manage me through this, aren't you? You're trying to act like some sort of love coach."

"All I'm saying is that maybe you should stop settling for everything that comes your way. Reach a little harder. Or maybe work on the technique. Your last two girlfriends, Cherry and Mary, were you the one who asked them out? Did you even protest when they left?"

"Their names were Marie and Cheryl. They were fine people, but I was drinking a lot. They wanted to help me. I wasn't good for them."

"You *were* a sorry shit, but you got over it. Who is this new one, anyway?"

Adam hesitated again.

"Actually, you've met her. She was the neurologist who took care of you when we got in that car accident."

Serge paused, astonished. "How did that—? When did—?" He stopped again.

"Yeah," said Adam.

He snorted and looked down.

"I wish I remembered her better. She was a brunette, right?"

"Well, it's over. Is that really your whole plan, Serge? Life of leisure and maybe work at your parents' restaurant? Do you want a family? Kids?" Adam asked, trying to change the subject.

Serge waved his hand. "There is time to figure it all out."

"We could be fired at any moment."

"You have *some* savings and investments. You're large. You can work the farm. Or as a bouncer."

Well, at least Serge's suggestions made more sense than the career test.

"I'm trying to *visualize*, as you like to put it, my future, Serge. I'm tired of finding crappy new apartments, tired of trying to make new friends, tired of icing my leg, downing ibuprofen, bruises, stitches. I don't think I like hockey anymore, Serge. That's what I'm trying to tell you."

He stopped. He didn't think he'd ever said it out loud before.

"Well, I don't like every single minute of it either, especially the waiting," Serge said, "but most people don't like what they do for a living. My brother, he works in the office and plays the accordion in a zydeco band at night. Is he happy? No, he is not happy. But he cannot play the accordion for a living. He is not as hopeless as the washboard player in that band – I mean, the washboard? – but still, the accordion is a difficult mistress."

"I can't even play the washboard, Serge."

"It will all work out."

"How can you—"

"The rest of my life will not be as good as this, Adam. I may not be very good at the hockey, I may not appear in any record books or earn lots of money, but in my hometown, every time I go home, they unfold a banner with my name on it, and children at the high school gymnasium come up to me and ask me to be in their pictures. My parents are proud of me because I am on an NHL team. It doesn't matter how bad it is. I just never thought I'd see the day. So you can cluck and worry and feel as dissatisfied as you want. I am going to enjoy it while it lasts."

–

Harry Frobisher lay heavily sedated in an Okanagan hospital with a fractured hip.

Helen had gotten her long, bumpy nose from him, her cold hands, and her hardheadedness. Or at least she thought she had received that last gift. She wanted to run from the hospital hallway, run out of the town, and back all the way to her living room, to her couch. She had gotten her long legs from her father, too – all the better for dashing away.

Her mother was sitting stiffly by the hospital bed, eyes glued to a television. Helen and her brother, Stephen, hovered outside the room.

She was done firing questions at the doctors, done watching, and talking.

She massaged her temples and practiced her deep breathing again.

He was going to be fine. He'd broken his hip, that was all. There was no need to have a meltdown. The course of his illness was completely typical of a patient with advanced parkinsonism. He would probably be in the hospital for a while. There was no need for her to lose her shit.

But her brother was talking to her about the possibility of sending him to an assisted living facility. She should have supported it. She *did* support it – the logical part of her brain did. It was really better for everyone. But she still didn't want to say it out loud, because agreeing meant admitting that Harry Frobisher was not going to improve.

She wanted to put her fists over her ears and stop listening.

She was used to taking control. But there was nothing she could do here. The doctors were fine, attentive, motivated, and even sympathetic. Her father knew most of them. They all knew him.

She remembered the first time he had taken her to the hospital. She must have been about five years old. She had loved it from the start. The clean, wide hallways, the scrubs and white coats. She loved the lines on the floors, telling her where to walk in order to get to the wards. She spent a lot of time skipping along those lines. Her favorite thing, though, was following her father around. He wore a suit and tie underneath his coat, and he let her listen to his stethoscope. He introduced her to everyone, and she loved the attention they bestowed on Dr. Frobisher's kid. She was still young enough that she didn't know that she was a curiosity – Dr. Frobisher's half-Chinese child. Someone usually made a variation on the same jokes: "Oh, I see you have a new resident following you!" or "Did you bring along a second opinion?"

Stephen was eight. He found the whole thing humiliating.

Helen returned to the hospital with a plan. The next time someone asked if she was the newest addition to the department, she was ready. "I'll be rounding with Dr. Frobisher in fifteen minutes," she said.

Harry had coached her and helped her a bit – a lot – with word choice, but the idea had been hers and hers alone.

When someone asked if she was the second opinion, she said, "My colleague here—" she would indicate Harry, "and I, we're about to discuss a course of treatment."

The nurses and doctors who laughed and played along with her, she liked. The ones who patted Helen on the head and asked Harry how old she was, she didn't. She was old enough that she knew they were trying to put her in her place, but not quite old enough to figure out how to put that into words.

One day, she would know a lot of things, she'd told herself. One day, she'd have all the answers, just like Dad did.

Except, staring at her father, she realized that despite the fact that she was a grown woman with a medical degree, she still didn't know anything.

"I don't want to do this," she said to Stephen. "I know it's the right thing to do, but I... can't."

"Helen, you're going to have to do better than that," Stephen said in his bossy older sibling voice. "Mum can't handle this by herself."

She wanted to insist that she knew things that Stephen didn't. She wanted to summon up a vast store of knowledge and floor him with statistics and treatment options. But she'd always looked up to him, and he knew it. She had no authority with him.

"Helen, it hasn't failed to escape my notice that you just haven't been coming up as often."

Helen muttered something about establishing her practice and hospital shifts.

"Bullshit," said Stephen. "You still managed to come when you were dancing. You drove up all the time during med school and residency."

Helen's older brother, Stephen, was a professor of Romance languages. His partner, Gordon, was in the chemistry department. It was a joke waiting to be made.

"And when you're here," Stephen continued, "you spend more time quibbling over dosage with Dad's doctors than you do talking with us."

They glared at each other. Or rather, Stephen glowered at her, and she pouted at his reflection in the window.

"We aren't doing this. We aren't going to fall into our old roles again," he said.

"At least I know about the disease." Even as she said it, she knew how false that was.

"You may know about medicine, but you don't know what it's like for Mum or, for that matter, Dad. Staying there is bad for them. I know you don't like the idea of selling, but Mum feels bad enough about it as it is. You need to summon up just a bit of support. There are stairs; there aren't any handrails. There are only two bathrooms in that old house, and they're narrow and easy to slip in. They stove is tricky; the porch is rickety; their driveway is way too long to shovel easily. Aside from that, Mum is isolated. She doesn't go out. She doesn't have the time."

"She never did that much before."

"Well that's because she's never liked living there, anyway. We're gone, and she doesn't have that many friends. Even after more than thirty years there, she's still seen as an interloper, that Chinese woman who married the town's bachelor doctor. I mean, never mind that her aunt ran the laundry in town for fifty years. Never mind that she was born the next town over and she sounds exactly like everyone else."

"It was nowhere near as bad as you say. I never noticed that stuff."

But of course Helen knew that was a lie. Stephen's own youth hockey team had tried to take him out, after all. She closed her eyes to the memory.

"It wasn't bad for you. You were a girl, and you never had to be a teenager there. You left for ballet school before people could really do horrible things to you. And you weren't queer."

Stephen rubbed the scar on his cheek and gave a short laugh. "Anyone who thinks the Asian experience in North America is a monolith should come look at our family." He shook his head. "Listen, your experience was different from mine, Helen. And neither of us has any idea what Mum's has been like. Though God knows, she never made it easier for herself or for us."

"But Mum has lived there a long time, Stephen. People are different now. The population has changed. I saw an Indian restaurant on Main Street."

"That's not the point. We're missing the point." Stephen scrubbed his face. "If they move," he said more quietly, "they'll be near me, Helen. I'll be able to get up quickly for emergencies. This is all stuff you already know. Helen, you know this is better."

"He's still got some of his faculties. He doesn't talk as much and he isn't as active, but he *knows*, Stephen. It's all locked up in an uncooperative body. It's breaking his heart."

She was not going to cry. She was not.

"Do you remember when we were little, little kids," she said, "we used to hide his ties, because we knew he wouldn't go out without one? And we wanted him to stay at home a little longer. But he'd always find them within five minutes, no matter how clever we tried to be, no matter how deeply we thought we concealed them? And he'd always put them back in exactly the same place, and the next morning, we'd do it again. He knew that we were going to run off with them. There's no way he didn't know. And he let us do it anyway. He never yelled at us; he never even looked frustrated. He'd just lope around the house in his very proper, perfectly pressed trousers, crouching to look in cupboards or on shelves."

Stephen smiled grimly. "And he'd call out for them, too. *Oxford stripe! Oxy! Paisley! Where are you?* It's a good thing we never thought to separate the herd."

"We thought about it. You were smart, though. You knew just how far to push it."

He put his arm around her.

"Helen, what's going on with you? As you like to point out, you're around sick people all the time. I just don't understand. I guess I thought that you'd be better at—"

She stiffened, not wanting to hear any more. She wanted to shove herself out of Stephen's arms.

Luckily, the clack of footsteps announced Gordon's arrival.

"You guys, how is he?"

Her brother-in-law kissed Helen on the forehead and reached over to flick a piece of lint from Stephen's shoulder.

"He's the same," Stephen said, into Helen's hair. She unloosed herself from his grip. "We should probably go eat something, maybe, see if Mum wants to come, or pick something up for her."

Gordie drove them to a pub near the hospital. Helen was glad he was there. He chattered tactfully while Stephen picked at his turkey club. The mood that she and Stephen had established briefly, the complicity of two children, was broken.

Gordie was telling them about how the new associate professor in his department apparently had made a Twitter account to post chemistry jokes and rude pictures of himself. All of his students followed it.

Helen spied a hockey game on the TV. She could pick out Oregon's blue and gold uniforms. She didn't know which team they were playing. It hardly mattered. She never paid attention to the games much beyond thinking about the physical impact the players' bodies made against each other. And, of course, Adam. She breathed in the beery air of the wood-paneled room and turned her fork over in the chicken Caesar salad. Her eyes drifted back to the television. She couldn't tell if he was on the ice. That meant he probably wasn't.

Stephen was asking if she wanted another beer. She shook her head and tried to concentrate. She was tired. She hadn't slept much on the plane, and she had been at the hospital all day. She couldn't wait to get back in the car, pick up her mother, and drive back home and sleep in a real bed.

And there he was: Adam. With a shiver, she gazed at the screen. He coasted around on the ice. She knew him despite the helmet, despite the other players drifting in front of him. She wanted to shake them away impatiently. She wanted to clear away the waitress, who stood in front of her to deliver another beer to Stephen. She wanted to walk right up to the television and stare at Adam Magnus and have him stare back at her.

The blow seemed to come out of nowhere.

Suddenly he was falling and then skating forward with fury. Another player entered the brawl, and another, and another. He was buried under a pile of flailing bodies. She could see the blood streaking the ice.

Helen couldn't tear her eyes away from the screen. She made a small moan.

"Helen?" Gordie asked.

She couldn't say anything. What could she say? She was angry with Adam – and scared for him. And most of all, she could not think of why he would do that to himself.

Stephen glanced at her and at the screen. *He* wasn't upset by the sight of a hockey game. He didn't make the connection. "You're tired. Let's go get Mum and go home," Stephen said, taking out his wallet.

She wanted to protest. He hadn't finished eating. But he left money on the table and steered her out of the pub. In the cold, wet air, she found that she was able to breathe again.

Gordie sprinted off to get the car while Stephen and Helen stood in the rain.

"So Helen, have you given any more thought to the assisted living facility?"

"You're right, of course," she said robotically.

"So that's it. We're going to put him on the waiting list now if we want to be able to do this."

Helen stayed silent.

Stephen rubbed his face and sighed. Her handsome brother. She didn't think much about how hard growing up must have been for him. She'd only thought about how

Mum favored him, the son. But no one had made it easy for him.

He looked older. But he and Gordie, they were wonderful and at ease with each other. She wondered if she would ever find that.

"Look, I know it's hard for you, Helen. It's hard on all of us. But Mum and I have talked a lot about this. Dad, too. We're doing this with or without you. The decision's been made. We're all just going to have to get used to it. It'll be easier on you if you can just let it go."

He sighed and hugged her to him. She let him. It was the most she could manage.

Chapter Six

Drop the Puck! Should Portland Ban Hockey?

Helen hated her title.

She'd written the damn article when she arrived back in Portland after the frustrating trip to Canada. She signed her name and e-mailed it in to the *Portland Tribune*.

Ah well, it was only the op-ed page. Even better, it was in a newspaper. No one read newspapers anymore.

She believed every word she'd set down. She'd tried to be thoughtful. She'd tried to marshal her arguments in a completely logical way, but she was fooling herself that they were lined up like perfect soldiers. Because, the truth was, seeing Adam go down had made her feel helpless, and the helplessness made her furious with him. She was not supposed to feel anything about him. He was practically a stranger – a stranger whose injuries she was now obsessed with checking. He'd injured his knee, was all she could find out, but she knew there was more that hadn't been reported. She'd seen blood.

It was entirely possible, Helen thought, that she was writing about the ravages of post-concussive trauma in order to avoid dealing with her father and the rest of her family. It was entirely possible, too, that she was doing this because in this case, she could actually do something, anything.

Depression. Explosivity. Aggression. Dementia.

Her father exhibited all of those signs at times. Then again, so did she, lately.

She pushed back her hair and tried to concentrate on patient notes, but her fingers were restless.

She stood up. Head trauma was preventable, she repeated to herself, swinging her arms around as she paced behind her desk. It was something that people could avoid if their sports didn't involve shoving, punching, and sticks. *Depression. Explosivity. Aggression. Dementia.*

How terrible it would be if that happened to Adam. *Or anyone else.*

It wasn't that she had feelings for him, of course. He was a smart guy. He was, actually, great and unexpectedly funny, and – she faltered – really kind. And sexy – the courteousness was sexy (as were his shoulders). It was strange to think of that person, that gentle, alert person, getting into brawls. She'd hated watching him get pummeled that night and on all the other nights. Not because she cared for him, not that way. (Or rather, yes, she did care, because she was a doctor, and she always cared about helping people.) But she didn't *like* him, not more than it was normal to like someone that she'd met and talked to and laughed with, someone who had stripped off her clothes and made her voice go hoarse, someone who had been so unexpected, so different from what she had imagined.

But it wasn't like she could exactly deliver the message to him in person. Or that she wanted to.

Yes, on a few nights, in her parents' home, in her old twin bed, she had thought of his freckled nose at her chest as his teeth pulled gently on her nipple. She'd slid her hands underneath the waistband of her flannel pajamas, wishing that she felt his big fingers tracing her wetness. The sounds he made when he pushed inside her... She'd thought she preferred silence from the men she slept with, but she had been wrong. Every small sound that escaped him, every pant, every click of his throat, made her wild. She was amazed that she was the one who was making him groan. She was the one who was making this big, stoic man lose control. And the knowledge had driven her nearly out of her mind with excitement.

She knew she was not being rational. Yes, this was just one big way of escaping the reality about the house, her mother, her brother, and most important, her father, but that didn't seem to make her able to shake her thoughts. She couldn't do anything about Harry, but she could certainly stir up some public opinion. Maybe even help Adam avoid a similar fate. Not that it was personal.

At least she could do this one thing. She could write about this one thing that could prevent one person from all of this grief – all of her grief. She was not completely helpless.

She had sat with her father, finally, before she left. She held his hand for a while and tried to talk with him. "How are your friends?" he asked in this new, thick, slow voice of his. "Are you still dancing?"

"I thought you hated going to recitals, Dad," she said lightly.

He shook his head slowly. "All those cute little girls falling over like ducks," he said.

But he was woozy and drifting in and out. The space between each word became longer and longer. She wasn't even sure if he was remembering the past or if he was just in the past.

She shook her head. He wasn't as far gone as that. It was the drugs talking. She checked the dosage and looked at his worn, white face.

"All of you in feathers," he said.

Her very first recital. "We were dressed as swans."

But he had fallen asleep.

–

The Tribune called Helen the next day to fact-check everything.

She was sitting in her tiny office at the Pearl District practice. She gave a little whoop that they were really running it and then a shudder when she hung up the phone. They had e-mailed a draft back to her, bristling with corrections and queries. It was horrible. Why was she doing this?

"What's that about?" asked the receptionist, Joanie, lounging in the doorway.

"An op-ed I wrote is going to be published in the *Trib* tomorrow," said Helen. "If I can change all this stuff." She gestured to the screen.

"You mean like in the newspaper?"

"It'll be online, too," said Helen.

Joanie looked slightly affronted. "I'll pick up a few copies for the office tomorrow," she said, turning on her heel.

Helen sighed. Joanie read a lot – a lot more than Helen did, for sure. She always had a paperback going. Right now, she was in the middle of P. G. Wodehouse. In her off hours, she was an actor in an experimental theater group. Helen thought of her own sad tablet PC, queued up with monographs and *NEJM* articles. Concussion, chronic traumatic encephalopathy, Parkinson's, and parkinsonism. *Brains.* That was her rich mental life.

She began checking through the queries that the newspaper editor had e-mailed her. Pretty soon, Petra and Sarah were jostling like toddlers through the doorway.

"What's the op-ed piece about?" Sarah asked, plunking herself down in a chair.

Petra hovered behind her.

"Don't you have appointments?" Helen asked.

"Don't you?" Sarah asked.

"Is Joanie a little miffed at me?" Helen asked Petra.

Sarah answered. "She's used to working for a bunch of condescending shits. Come on, what's this thing about?"

"I call for a ban on hockey. I'm a concerned neurologist. The head injuries make it inexcusable."

Petra stirred a little, and Helen avoided looking at her. She knew Petra suspected she was going off the deep end. Maybe she was.

Luckily, Sarah was bumping in her seat. "Wow, ambitious much?"

"Not really. Chronic traumatic encephalopathy, or CTE, has been in the news for football players lately, but we've got an at-risk hockey team. It's a local story."

"You don't mind being used as anti-Yevgeny fodder?" Sarah asked.

"What's that supposed to mean?"

"I mean, the guys who oppose the new arena and that Russian billionaire owner – Yevgeny Molotov – are just going to use this as more proof that we have to drum the Wolves out of town."

"They're separate issues."

"The team's controversial, and as a result, your argument's going to be leverage."

Helen sighed. "Look, I'm not taking a political stance about the arena. I don't know enough about it. What I do know is that concussion is associated with dementia, and it's entirely preventable. To me, it's black and white."

"That's unlike you," Petra murmured.

"You're right," Sarah said cheerily. "Black and white sounds so much more like me. God knows, I'm all for preventive medicine, and I hate it when people do stupid things that make them stupider all the time. The world would be so much more orderly if we were all more conscious and responsible and ate our kale. But at the same time, *hockey*. Something about all that male aggression and sweating and well-defined goals. On ice! I'm a convert."

"How can you be so flippant about this?" Helen asked. She was starting to clench her fists.

"Where better to have chaos than in an organized team sport where everyone knows the rules and the risks?"

"I don't think that people do understand the risks. The bulk of our understanding about CTE has been accumulated fairly recently. We only really began to think about it through football players. We haven't even begun to think about hockey."

"Cars kill more people than hockey. Are we going to ban those?" Sarah asked, adopting the furrowed brow and carrying tones of what Helen recognized as the Sarah-Argument-Stance.

Petra groaned.

"We have licensing and safeguards, safety features that we're always refining, and a police force. Besides, more people do understand the risks of driving. Not a fair comparison."

"You're right, it's not very fair," Sarah said, her feet swinging. She was a little too short for the chair. "But it's not a bad comparison. Most people don't understand the risks involved in driving. Otherwise, they wouldn't do it. Moreover, as you said, data's still early on hockey *specifically*. Unless you can provide longer-term studies, the link between CTE and playing, skating around, and shooting pucks is tenuous. The problem is the fighting, and even then, it's more about the long-term effects of fighting. But continuous brawls aren't the whole sport – it's just the way it's played in certain moments. You can't just call for an outright ban. That's painting with a broad brush, where a finer will do." Sarah jumped up. "I've got an appointment in five. Got to review notes."

Helen watched after her. "I should know better than to get into arguments with her."

Petra nodded. "At least there's no splatter pattern to clean up this time."

Helen nodded. "I figure it's good practice to spar with her if letters to the editor start coming in."

Petra lingered. "How's your dad?"

"It's a fracture. Doctor says to expect another week in hospital." Helen hesitated. "They're moving him to a rehabilitation facility, then long-term assisted care. In Vancouver. My mother will move in with Stephen and Gordon until the house sells or she finds a place of her own."

She hadn't talked with Petra or Sarah much about her father's illness. They knew he had parkinsonism, but the subject was too raw, too painful for her. She wondered how much Petra had guessed. "They've had this in the works for a while," Helen added. "The fall just precipitated everything. There was nothing I could do, so I left."

"Right," said Petra. "And this thing with the hockey."

"What about it?"

"This whole thing, this campaign, this stance. It isn't like you, Helen."

"What isn't like me, Pete? To be decisive, to take action?"

"To declare something is black and white when, clearly, you have mixed feelings. To take a stance on, of all things, hockey?"

"I do know a few things about the sport. And what I do know isn't good."

Petra shook her head. "Adam Magnus," Petra said.

"What about him?"

"Did you talk to him about this, before you wrote it?"

"No, I didn't."

"You do realize that you've basically said that the man should be out of a job."

"Well, since I don't expect to ever see him again, I guess I'll be fine."

"Portland is kind of a small town, in a way."

"I'm from a small town. Portland is nothing like small."

"So this thing, this interest in hockey—"

"It's concussion. I'm a neurologist. My brother played hockey, and it was brutal. It's not a sudden interest. It's just stuff coming together."

"Well, I'm an allergist, and it's *my* training to look at outsize reactions to sometimes harmless stimuli. Are you sure that your interest in hockey and concussion has nothing to do with Adam?"

"It's not personal. I try to help everyone."

"And this behavior has nothing to do with your dad's brain injury? It's not a manifestation of all the stress you're under?"

"It's not a behavior. It's genuine concern," said Helen. "I'm fine. *I'm fine.*"

"If you say so."

–

The Wolves had won. They had actually gotten ahead by a goal and stayed that way by the time the buzzer sounded.

There had even been a short fight — enough to make Adam seem useful. It was still hard, though. He shouldn't complain. Aside from a few bruises and the strain to his trick knee, he was all right. Plus, he'd forgotten how good it felt after a win, the sound of sticks falling to the ice as grown men let go, slapped backs, whooped and hollered, piled up on Serge. The high lasted all the way back on the plane ride home, through the time Adam dropped his luggage and looked around his apartment and sighed in contentment. Maybe he could keep this, he thought. Maybe they would continue, he could retire on some sort of medium note, and he could get a job coaching a minor league team. Maybe he could even find something around here, and he would be able to stay in this city, have some sort of normal, enjoyable life. Modest goals seemed suddenly within reach.

He decided to go for a run along the waterfront. It was raining, but he didn't mind. That was another thing he loved about this place. He didn't mind cold. He had grown up in cold, in dry, sunny, frigid country. The rain was bracing and he liked to watch it from his big window, and he enjoyed being out in it, with the water slapping across his face. He was doing something, really just sparring with the elements, a battle without actual rancor or hard feelings, just good fun for everyone.

He came back, drenched and happy. He still had to go in for a medical check and to work on weights. Matt, his trainer, was concerned that he was getting too lean. But Adam didn't want any more bulk.

His phone rang. It was Serge. He sounded slightly alarmed.

"Your girlfriend, Dr. Helen Chang Frobisher—"

Adam's heart stopped. "What happened to her?"

A nervous laugh. "Relax, she's all right. Well, except she might have Yevgeny's goons after her, if his people bother to read the newspapers."

Adam did not quite relax. "What do you mean?"

"She says we should be run out of town. It's in the *Tribune*. I have a news alert about the team set up for my phone."

"Are you sure it's her? How do you even remember her name?"

"Helen Chang Frobisher, Portland neurologist. *Your lady love.* It's her."

Adam opened his laptop and found the newspaper's website. He looked through the sports section. Nothing.

"Are you sure? I don't see it."

"It ran on the opinion pages. I doubt anyone will pay attention to it, but Adam, are you sure she was okay with your leaving? Or were you such a lousy lay?"

"She left me," Adam said, gritting his teeth.

He found the page.

Serge laughed. "So I guess it was option b, then."

"I. Was. Not. Lousy."

And there it was, her name in the opinion pages.

He could hear her clipped voice in his ears, explaining the symptoms, laying out in ruthless detail all the things that could happen to a body during the course of a hockey season. He could see her hands, slicing the air for emphasis.

"Well, it's not a love letter, this little piece, and the medical stuff isn't news to any of us," Serge said. "The anti-arena people might latch on to it, though. Although, it does send chills through me when she writes that physicians aren't sure how many concussions or micro concussions are too many. Until it's too late. We've all been in the fights. Sooner or later, we start losing the words, forgetting, getting depressed. It starts making you a little, I don't know, paranoid, you know." A pause. Serge asked, "Is paranoia one of the symptoms?"

Adam was reading quickly now.

> Depression, explosive temper, short-term memory loss, word-finding difficulty, aggression.

He was having almost all of those symptoms right now. First she'd fled his bed, and now she was insulting his profession in public. He was an adult – he knew what the stakes were, and he had made a choice. And here was Helen Frobisher treating him like a know-nothing child who couldn't keep himself safe. Clearly, she had no respect for him at all, and he was furious. He had no words to say how angry he was. And above all, he was having trouble remembering why he had liked Helen Frobisher at all.

Chapter Seven

Helen was sitting in Stream on Friday night, thinking about the last time she'd been here. Petra was sticking her tongue out at Ian. Ian was saying something ridiculous and affectionate, and Helen was wishing that her drink would just hurry up and arrive.

Instead, Adam Magnus stormed in looking furious and magnificent, and for a moment, the room went still. As his eyes scanned the room, Helen noticed the bruise right across his cheekbone, the short, golden hair, and icy eyes. Anger lit his whole body like a filament. She couldn't look away.

Sensing trouble, Ian stood up, but Helen barely noticed him. He was a tall man. Adam was taller.

He was incandescent. He was glowering.

He was looking right at her.

Her heart started racing. And, oh lord, she did not just lick her lips, did she? But here she was, gazing up at the six-foot-plus-infinity inches of the blazing glory that was Adam Magnus, and her tongue once again traveled the perimeter of her mouth because suddenly she was parched from looking at the hot fury of this sun.

His steps toward her were light.

"Helen Frobisher, we need to talk."

"I can't. My—"

"You. Me. *Now.*"

"In a public place? You want to make a scene?"

"A newspaper is pretty much the damn definition of public, Helen. *You started it.*"

The last was in another low rumble that made her entire body tingle down to her toes. She squirmed uneasily, and he leaned in closer.

Beside Helen, Petra cleared her throat. "Hey," she said.

And because, despite his fury, he was a polite Minnesota farm boy, Adam dragged his eyes over to Petra and said curtly, "Hi. I'm Adam."

A giggle escaped Petra's lips. "Don't you mean, *Madam, I'm Adam?*"

"Pete," Ian said, low.

But Adam had caught Petra in his burning glare. "Are you making fun of me?"

Petra shrank back. Ian narrowed his eyes.

Helen said, hastily, "I think she's just trying to deflect attention."

"With palindromes?" Adam said.

Petra said, slightly disappointed, "Oh, you've heard that one already?"

He didn't really answer.

His shoulders were still tensed, and his eyes still angry and – Helen swallowed – hurt. But he was looking around now, as if he was conscious of the stir he'd made and how large he loomed. He was trying to contain his fury, Helen realized. Another man would have just let it loose, not caring. But even in his anger, he was so... *considerate.*

Ian motioned for him to sit and signaled someone to bring them drinks. Adam's eyes glittered, and he looked like he could use a dash of cold water.

He slid in next to Helen. He was hot – seething – and she felt herself go warm.

Far from being intimidated, Petra was looking from Helen's face to Adam's, like an eager bird, a glint of speculation in her eye. Helen wanted to kick her friend under the table, but Adam was crowding her so much that he would have detected any movement.

"Let's start again," Helen said. "How've you been?"

He glared.

The silence was a little uncomfortable.

The drinks and some food came, luckily, and Petra abandoned her scrutiny to say something to Ian.

"May I ask you why you seem to want to put me out of a job?" Adam asked quietly.

And somehow, the quietness of the question, the way he'd contained himself only to have all that sadness leak out was the worst of all.

"It's not about you," Helen said. She took a big swallow of her white wine.

His eyes were searching her, and she turned even redder. There were so many reasons why he was wrong for her. Most of all, it was because he made her feel too many things all at once. She was hot and uncomfortable. She also felt guilty, more so because he was looking at her like *that*, like she was the one who had punched him in the face and left that bruise on his cheekbone. Yes, she had realized intellectually that a call for banning hockey meant that she supported the dismantling of sports teams, the outlawing of the NHL, the dissolution of camps and schools, stores, and an entire community.

But she hadn't really, really expected anyone to take her seriously. Except this was Portland, the land where quixotic quests were no longer quixotic. While the town might not be able to get rid of all hockey, there were some who were raring to get rid of the arena, the Wolves, and, by extension, Adam Magnus.

And yes, although she had told herself that she had thought this through, and weighed the consequences, she hadn't actually thought far enough or near enough. She hadn't thought of this person, sitting next to her, whom she knew up close.

Not very sporting of her.

So, of course, she said, "I hope you don't expect an apology."

Petra groaned.

"An apology is what I expect for your sneaking out after that night, after making it clear you wouldn't. For this, though? For this, I don't even know what this is."

"It's actually a way to keep you safe," she said.

Petra snorted.

"What?" Helen asked, her hands flying out. She almost knocked over her wineglass. "I'm a neurologist. You can't expect me to support something that involves so many knocks to the head."

She was losing control of her limbs and her brain. Best stick to the message.

"I'm not asking you to apologize," Adam said, tightly, "or to justify it medically. I'm not asking you to do anything. I just want to know why this, why now? You could have done this before you met me, or you could have said nothing. But instead, you waited until after…"

After.

Out of the corner of her eye, Helen could see that Petra was about to open her mouth again, but Ian settled his hand on her shoulder. He whispered something.

"Ian just told me to butt out," Petra announced. "We're going to the bar."

When they were safely away, Helen scooted away from Adam, but he followed her, sliding after her on the seat. Clearly, it was physical intimidation, something he had no doubt mastered. "You don't have to shadow me like that," she said irritably. "I'm not making a quick getaway."

"Right, because you only bolt after sex."

"I was trying to spare you—"

"That is such utter and complete *bullshit*," he growled so low and intense that the table rattled under her fingers and the sound seemed to be sucked from the room.

His last words delivered in that whisper roared so close to her ear that she could feel the warm force of his breath drive at her. Helen's face and neck and chest prickled with fear and… something else, and she saw her fingertips grip a fork so tightly that her knuckles went white. But what she really wanted to do was turn around and kiss him, to touch him right there on his firm, broad chest. She could see it was still tense and bunched, moving up and down. She wanted to soothe him.

Adam angry was really, really something.

–

He was on the edge. His hands were gripping the seat so tightly that he doubted that the leather was ever going to recover. And she was sitting there, staring at his chest like she wanted to lick it. Arousal and anger battled so ferociously in him that he let out a snarl that lifted a loose wisp of her hair, and that wisp drifted toward him – as she *drifted* toward him and righted herself with a jerk.

She took a gulp of wine, and Adam enjoyed a rare moment of feeling like he was the only one who wasn't in control.

He scrubbed his hands through his hair and wished for a moment that it were longer, so that he could grip it hard and pull it. From the way Helen tracked his hands, it seemed she was having similar thoughts.

He wanted to make her look straight at him. He wanted to pull her chin right toward him and make those brown eyes widen, and he wanted to listen as her breath came faster and faster. Instead, he put his hands down flat on the table. "Do you blame me for being angry? What the fuck do you think you were doing?"

She wriggled a bit more. "Look, maybe it was terrible of me to have left without waking you—"

"That is not what I'm talking about, Helen. That is not the point."

"But you were asleep, and I did have rounds. I had to go home and pull on some fresh clothing."

"You're avoiding the goddamn fucking issue."

He heard her sharp intake of breath. "Damn right I'm avoiding the issue," she snapped.

Then she slumped. "It's what I do best."

This was not going as planned.

He had intended to find her, be furious with her, and get her to admit she was wrong. A minor offshoot of this plan had been to bring her home to his apartment to have crazy sex and, the next morning, pancakes.

He even had syrup.

But part of that scenario was that he was going to feel better and satisfied with what she had to tell him. That the whole thing was going to disappear or that some other Portland neurologist named Helen Chang Frobisher had written the thing. But he'd tried to forget that this was Helen. Difficult, annoying, stubborn, dizzyingly beautiful Helen. She had no doppelgangers. She made no apologies. He would not be satisfied. She was giving him a headache. She'd probably gone into doctoring because she caused so many of them.

How did she do that to him? How did she twist him up like that, making him angry and hungry and guilty within the space of minutes? He wanted to slam his fists down on the table with all the various and at odds feelings suppressed in his muscles, but he knew he couldn't. It always scared people, and right now, although he was angry, he didn't want to scare her.

He breathed through his nose a couple of times and relaxed his shoulders and hands. He had to say it all. He had to let it out before it strangled him. "I don't know what's going on with you, Helen. Maybe I don't even care anymore. We don't know each other that well. But let me spell it out for you: This thing hurts the team I play on and it hurts the team's case for staying here in Portland. You may think this is a one-off thing, a doc just giving an opinion in a paper that no one reads. But that's not the only thing at play here. It's just one more blow to an already fragile system – a hit from an unexpected direction, the kind of jolt that makes my teeth rattle. So yeah, this endangers my job, which is already hanging by a thread. It also means you dislike the thing that I do for a living and, in a way, you dislike me."

Out of the corner of his eye, he saw her mouth open. But he didn't care. "It may seem like a small thing, but it was personal. You hurt me in so many ways. You fucking screwed me over in so many goddamn ways, Helen Frobisher. You may have hurt my livelihood. It's not your fault entirely that my life is not ideal at the moment. For a while, you even made my life seem better. But… there it is, damaged. And you can't even apologize to me. You can't even meet my eye."

He was right, and it made his heart sore. She didn't say sorry. She didn't meet his eye. She looked at the table.

He got up and left.

–

Well, that could not have possibly gone worse, Helen thought, crouched in her shower stall, as if the shower curtain could shield her from her own messes.

She was terrible. Worse, *he* thought she was terrible. If she were simply losing her mental faculties and managed to hide it from the world, what would it matter? She could go madly and merrily on her way. But now, one person in the world had incontrovertible proof that she really wasn't doing very well.

Not very well at all.

She wished she had some popcorn. Sarah would probably gag if she could hear Helen's thoughts. Food! In a bathroom!

Well, most of Helen's thoughts would make Sarah gag.

Sometimes, it was good to talk to Sarah. She wasn't the most sympathetic person in the world. Sometimes, she wasn't very nice. But she could probably talk almost anyone off a ledge just by sheer force of will.

It was possible that Helen was on a ledge.

She pulled out her phone. There were five messages from Petra.

Without checking any of them, Helen texted:

AT HOME. I'M FINE.

Then she called Sarah.

"They named this one Sahara. Maybe I get a quarter of a point for this one," Sarah yelled into the phone. No *hello*, no *how are you*. Helen closed her eyes and began to laugh.

Sarah was always loud after a good birth. It was probably from shouting to be heard above the baby's cries. She also had a scoring system for baby names. She was determined to have her patients name a child after her.

"They probably won't name a kid after me, unless I assist them on multiple births," Sarah added. "I'm just going to have to work on getting some good breeders into my practice."

Helen felt better already. "How's the kid?" she said.

"Apgar nine. Nine pounds, five ounces. Big enough for the mom to receive lifelong sympathy, not big enough to put her in any real danger. Short labor, only minor tears. I feel so awesome. Hang on, let me get some juice."

Some coins clinked, and Helen heard the rumbling of a machine.

"So why are you still at the hospital?" Helen asked.

"I'm covering for Sharma Rai. One of her patients is probably going to pop in an hour or so. Friday nights are party time for the forty-weeks set."

Helen thought about this. "How do you do it, Sarah? How do you just keep on going cheerfully? How do you stay so sure of yourself?"

"There's always work."

"What if your inability to do what you're supposed to do is the problem?"

Helen could hear Sarah taking a large gulp. She gave a little sniff.

"Let me tell you about Sahara's mom, Le-Anna. Le-Anna is one of those patients, you know, the one for whom every minor thing possible goes wrong. Do you have those?"

"Yeah, I do."

"Well, first of all, the first few weeks, I kept accidentally calling her Le-Ann instead of Le-Anna. She came in on a day when my ultrasound equipment wasn't working – that was a terrible day. I couldn't find that speedy little heartbeat without prodding Le-Anna's belly like a horny dolphin. Then, the mom had a little bleeding and freaked out. We muffed up the timing of her glucose challenge, and she had to come in and drink that horrible sweet drink again. Just a bunch of little things, tiny little things that were not her fault, not my fault, but they just served to undermine the relationship sort of subtly. It was all enough to rattle even me. And you know what, that kid is fine and Le-Anna's happy and healthy. So, I look at the result. I don't look at every little thing I do wrong. And believe me, I know I do get a lot of things wrong." Sarah paused. "Did that help?"

"Not as much as I'd hoped."

Sarah accepted that by taking another long draught. Helen heard the can clank in the recycling bin. "Sarah, I can't believe you just chugged V8."

"I know. The salt."

Sarah continued with nary a pause. "Your problem, Helen, is that you work with too many people with chronic pain. It can make a person feel helpless."

Helen was quiet.

"I was in the lobby the other day," Sarah said. "Mother brought a newborn down to wait for her husband to bring the car around. Of course, people flocked around her. A woman was there with her elderly father, and she said to the mother, *Here's your baby at the beginning of her life, and here's my father at the end*. And of course, everyone cooed at that, even the old gentleman, but when you think about it, what an odd thing it was to say out loud – even in a hospital. The newborn made it okay, but usually we hate saying it. Her father was dying."

Helen clutched the shower curtain.

"My father is dying," Helen said.

She heard Sarah huff and breathe. "I'm sorry, sweetie."

And Helen wept.

Chapter Eight

He needed to stop thinking about her, Adam thought, hauling weights to his shoulders. Helen Frobisher was obviously too much trouble for him. She was complicated and volatile. To date, Helen Frobisher had:

Shone a flashlight into his eyes despite his protests.

Yelled at him on a city street.

Screwed him and left without a word.

Called for his profession to be dismantled.

When he left, her pixyish friend Petra had even followed him out and demanded to know what he'd said to her. He added, *Got yelled at by an angry elf* to his list of things he could lay at Helen's feet.

But even then, he couldn't dislike her. There was pain, fear, some strange unnamable force at work behind all of this gorgeous mayhem. He could see it all in her hands and face when she had looked up at him: the panic. He'd wanted to reach out to comfort her, but he'd known that if he did, they'd do the same things to each other again and again.

He wouldn't have minded some of the things that they did.

But the rest was a self-destructive cycle.

Good for you for confronting her then leaving, he thought, hating himself.

He replaced the weights and wiped the sweat off of them with his towel. He used to like training because it gave him time to think. He was paid to think, in a way. It was his private joke to himself. But lately, he'd had trouble getting his mind on the tasks ahead. Maybe too many knocks to the head *had* addled him, just as she'd predicted.

Or maybe the problem was that all of his thoughts these days were a collection of little phrases he wanted to tell her, snapshots of things he wanted to show her. And maybe that was the worst trap of all. He wanted to prove to her that he was worth something, that he shouldn't be discarded. And why was he even trying to do this now when he had been the one to walk out on her?

He heard a clank next to him, and he pulled out his earbuds. The Swede – or was it the Norwegian guy? – was doing weights. They nodded in greeting, and Adam went to the leg press machine and toggled the weights.

The problem was that the business wasn't separate from his fears about the future. He disagreed with Helen, but he was headed to the same conclusions she was, in a way: *He* couldn't keep playing. And now maybe someday he was going to lose his wits. Of course, they talked about concussion on the teams he'd played on – the doctors, the coaches, the managers all got very earnest looks on their faces. But he hadn't seriously considered it until Helen. He was going to have to save up for the possibility of debilitating illness on top of it all. So dreaming of lingering in bed with Helen on a Sunday morning, seeing her in sunlight as the light poured in from the huge windows of his apartment – that was out of the question. He needed fat numbers in his bank statement, offers of employment with thick benefits packages that would cushion his soon-to-be-arthritic joints. He could not afford to moon over fleeting images of sunlight in Portland, of Helen's hand resting gently on his chest, of her sleepy smile. It had never happened; it never would. And even if it did, it was impractical. It didn't matter if she was going through things. He was also going through things. And now he could add the inevitable deterioration of his brain to the circling drain of his hockey career.

A tap on his shoulder startled him.

"You are done?" the Swedish kid asked uncertainly.

Adam looked up at this young, hungry teammate. He was in the weight room all the time – every time Adam was here, at least, which was often – and he was probably desperate to keep his place on the team, desperate for the team to make it.

Adam nodded and got up. He'd lost count of his reps anyway. He would pay for that at practice.

Life without hockey, he thought, for the umpteenth time. What would that be like? Looking at it in the abstract, he felt an unexpected twitch of interest.

He walked out of the training room in search of his tablet computer.

–

The last thing Helen wanted to do was talk about hockey.

It was her own fault. She had fashioned the bomb and lobbed it, and she'd hurt Adam. She still believed she was right, but she didn't like that he didn't like her. And the consequence was that the producer of a local public access show wanted her to go on television and act like an expert who had the weight of righteous conviction behind her. She wasn't sure she had it in her.

The woman calling from the *Declan Quail Show* said the publicity from going on TV would help Helen's cause, but as far as Helen knew, no one ever watched Declan Quail. She threw herself anew into researching clinical trials and experimental Parkinson's drugs. Writing about concussion in athletes had been a temporary aberration, some misguided hope of being able to do something besides beat her fists on an unyielding wall.

Adam had been a temporary aberration.

A temporary aberration that nonetheless had made her step back and try to calm herself.

She told the woman that she had to see patients, and she spent some time evaluating a woman for migraine. She wrote up some notes and put in a call to a pharmacy. When she finally emerged to the waiting room, Sarah bounced up to her. "Joanie says some TV producer wants to talk to you."

A few patients swung their gazes her way. "Let's not talk about this now," Helen said. She grabbed a file.

"You're a slender girl," said Mrs. Martens. "You'll look just right on the television. They say it adds twenty pounds, you know."

Helen helped Mrs. Martens with her walker and ushered her into the office.

"How is the new medication working out?" Helen asked.

"Why do they want you to be on TV?"

"I wrote something about chronic traumatic enceph-alopathy," said Helen, hoping the words would stymie Mrs. Martens.

"Never heard of it," Mrs. Martens said. "You have to make sure they don't put too much makeup on you. Nowadays with the big screens and the HD, you really need to be careful about the foundation. Make sure they blend it into your neck."

The rest of the day did not get much better.

"You should go on! Think of the free publicity for the practice," said Sarah. "You should wear a T-shirt with our address."

"I can coach you on how to speak and how to act," offered Joanie.

"And although I promised to butt out of your life, and everyone else's," said Petra, "I can offer opinions if you want some."

There was a plea in Petra's eyes that said that she really, really wanted to be asked for opinions.

"You could become, like, our resident medical talking head," Sarah enthused. "You could get your own segment on the *Declan Quail Show*. You could bring me on to chat about the rate of C-sections in the greater Portland area."

"Why does everyone's brain turn to mush when we start talking about appearing on TV? It's a local show that no one watches!" Helen asked.

She very deliberately slung her yoga mat over her shoulder in order to hint to her friends that she was leaving.

"First hockey makes you stupid, then TV finishes you off," Sarah said. "That could be another topic for your segment!"

Office hours were over. Helen had been hoping to avoid her friends, but they clearly had things to say to her. They were clustered around the doorway of her office.

"I don't have a segment. I'm not going on the show. For that matter, I didn't think about hockey for more than twenty years. I plan to avoid it for the next twenty," she said, putting on her coat.

"I don't think *hockey* is the problem," Petra said, making air quotes.

"Butt out, Petra," Helen said.

"You're Canadian," said Sarah. "You aren't meant to leave hockey alone. Besides, you have to go on the show. You can't disappear on the subject. Then the hockey goons will win."

"There's so much in that comment, I can't even begin to unpack it. I thought you were opposed to bans," said Helen.

"I am. But I am also a person who believes firmly in the beauty and sanctity of debate. And publicity. I believe in publicity."

"I'm not the best representative of the practice," said Helen. "Joanie's got his number. *You* call Declan Quail. *You* be on the show."

She grabbed her bag and her yoga mat and went toward her door. Sarah still blocked her.

Helen sighed. "If you must know the truth, I don't really feel like defending my stance anymore."

"Wow, you're wussing out. I never thought you'd do that," Sarah said. "Besides, no one ever watches that show anyway."

"Reverse psychology isn't going to work on me."

"Do you really think concussion in athletes is preventable?"

"Yes."

Sarah asked, "Aren't you concerned about the players?"

Petra added, "You know, those hard-bodied men who are going to be wandering around confused and crazed in the future, no one to tuck in their messy hockey jerseys, no one to soothe their sculpted brows."

Helen pressed her lips together. "Yes. I admit, as a medical professional, I am concerned."

About one sculpted brow in particular.

Petra said, "You know, Adam Magnus wrote a rebuttal piece for a sports blog. I have an alert set up for his name now." She pulled out her phone and read,

> We could wrap ourselves in layers of rubber,
> but inevitably someone will find out they
> have a latex allergy.

"That is so true. Latex allergy is no joke."

Sarah peeked over Petra's shoulder. "Oh, and this:

> careful about clutching those pearls – you
> could end up strangling yourself.

You know, he's kind of clever in a goofy way, which is more than I can say for your editorial."

"Oh, that's... I don't need to hear any more." Helen felt a little hurt by Adam's words. She didn't even own pearls, let alone clutch them. And as for her friends' comments, well of course her editorial wasn't funny. Head injury was no joking matter! That was the point of the whole damn article. Helen shifted her yoga mat. "You were mad at him the other night at Stream, Petra."

"Well, you were both a little unreasonable," said Sarah.

"Have you been discussing me?"

"Duh."

She moved to sit behind Helen's desk.

"So let's plan strategy: Magnus is the quarry," Sarah said, tenting her fingers. "Obviously, you have to take him down to save him. Like a biologist with a giant tranquilizer gun." She put her feet on Helen's desk.

"Adam is not some dumb beast who I could take down easily. He could hold his own against anybody. Besides, like I said, I've sort of changed my mind a little."

Joanie, who'd been lingering near the doorway, spoke, "So go on, say your piece, say that you've changed your mind about some things. It's a chance to publicly alter your story. And get us free PR."

"I could do that," Helen mused. "I could temper what I said."

"TV hates temperance," Sarah snapped. She got up and into Helen's face. "Go hard, or go home."

–

TV was one thing, but radio – local public radio – was classy, wasn't it? She agreed to a radio interview partly to appease her coworkers and partly because it somehow felt safe – safer. There were advantages to it, too. She didn't have to wear a pantsuit or fiddle with her hair – her usual work uniform of a skirt and button-down was fine. She didn't have to sit on her hands, although she still had to be careful that she didn't knock over the bottle of water they'd given her.

Really. She was fine.

Lynn Murtelle, host of the *Lynn Murtelle Show*, gave her a vague smile and wave, as if she were sending Helen off on an ocean liner and they weren't crammed together in a small, cluttered studio.

Helen looked through her notes and cleared her throat as quietly as she could, whispering into her shoulder to test out her voice. She'd thought more about vocal fry in the last ten hours than ever before in her life.

Shuffling through her notes, she tried to banish her nervousness. It was important for her to be careful, dispassionate, scientific. Also, she didn't want to hurt Adam – not more than she had already. Maybe she could make it clear during the interview that the arena didn't matter to her at all, that the team and their competence or lack of it certainly wasn't in question. She was just a neurologist trying to protect brains.

Dispassionate, she repeated to herself. *Fair.* And not a word about the stupid arena.

The light came on, and Lynn Murtelle began to talk with her head crooked so that she didn't have to look at Helen. She began her opening spiel about the show and then began to talk about concussion.

The introduction, Helen realized, was almost her whole editorial, word for word.

Not that Helen had it memorized or anything.

"Of course, Dr. Frobisher's editorial comes at an important juncture during the debate about Molotov's arena," Murtelle was saying.

"I don't really have any opinions either way about the arena," Helen interrupted. "For me, it was really about the medical reality of concussion."

Good job not mentioning the a-word, doofus.

"Yes, well that's what your side of the arena debate is saying," Murtelle noted.

Maybe Helen shouldn't have interrupted because ten minutes in, the interview didn't really seem to be going that well, especially when they opened up the show to callers.

"We have someone special on the line."

That didn't sound good.

"His name is Adam Magnus, and he plays on the left wing for the Portland Wolves—"

"Oregon Wolves," Adam's voice corrected.

"No brain damage there, I see." Lynn giggled, her voice suddenly becoming warm.

The room filled with the sound of Adam's chuckle, and Helen stewed. What was he doing listening to public radio? What was he doing calling into her show? *What was he doing laughing at this woman's terrible joke?*

"I wouldn't say that," Adam was teasing back. "This is radio so you can't tell if I managed to tie my own shoes."

"Oh, I'm sure you could manage to find someone to tie your shoes anytime," Lynn purred.

The public radio host was *flirting* with Adam? How was it that Lynn Murtelle had more game than Helen? Was she really jealous of a fiftyish, sex kitten public radio personality?

"Psychomotor retardation doesn't often manifest right away," Helen said.

Well, that statement certainly caused some dead air.

At least it jolted Lynn back into action. "Mr. Magnus, Dr. Frobisher, you two have engaged in a sort of war of words across media platforms recently," she said.

"Just a local newspaper editorial—" Helen started to object.

"Blogs, Twitter," Lynn said. "The group No Arena Now has been signal boosting it."

"Well, I don't tweet."

"Mr. Magnus does."

"I have trouble following Twitter," Helen said.

"It takes a lot of concentration," said Adam. "Besides, I have a few years before my psychomotor retardation makes it difficult."

Helen let that slide. "I just object to saying it's a war of words across media platforms if it's just small-time local media – er, no offense Lynn – and Adam's the one chasing me around with quips and comments. If you hadn't responded, then no would even be talking about it today."

"Oh, so you've read them."

"No, but someone I know said you were making jokes."

"Dr. Frobisher..." Lynn said.

"So you're the only one who gets to be funny here?" Adam asked.

"Mr. Magnus..."

"I wasn't trying to be funny. There is not one funny goddamn word in my editorial. It's all completely serious."

"No, there was one funny part where one neuron starts talking to another neuron and—"

"Dr. Frobisher, Mr. Magnus, maybe we can—"

"It's an *illustration* of neurofibrillary tangle," Helen said hotly. "It was not *supposed* to be funny."

Adam chuckled again. *Chuckled*. Since when did he chuckle like some sort of benign giant? If the radio listeners could see what sort of devastating assassin he looked like, then they'd be intimidated. She wanted to reach across the phone lines and thwack him on the head. Maybe give him a neurofibrillary tangle of his own.

Lynn Murtelle had had enough of them. "Okay, let's get this back on track," the host said, steel in her voice. "Adam, maybe you could tell me a little bit about what fighting in a hockey game is like…"

By the end of the segment, Helen hadn't covered half of her notes, Lynn Murtelle hated her, and Adam came off as reasonable and in control. She came off as… well, probably as a shrew.

"The nerve of him, calling into my show," she fumed over the phone to Petra, as she walked around the parking lot near the radio station, looking for her car.

"To be fair, it's not your show, and you did call for the ban of his sport," Petra said, mildly.

"Not you, too. I can at least understand it from Sarah."

"Oh, no. Don't lump me in with Sarah. I just mean that you can't control what other people say about things you put in public—"

"It was an editorial in a *newspaper*! Who the fuck reads the paper anymore, aside from public radio hosts?"

"And really, frankly," Petra continued, ignoring Helen, "when it comes to this, you can't expect Adam Magnus to agree with you."

"I wish he would," Helen muttered.

"I'm sure there are other ways you could convince him."

"*Petra.*"

"What? He likes you. You like him."

"I don't anymore. And he certainly does not like me at all at this point. Why are we even talking about this? I doubt I'll ever see him or hear from him again. Which is fine. I said my piece. Sort of. And that's done. I am never, ever doing that again. Now where the fuck is my car?"

Chapter Nine

So, it turned out Helen was going on TV after all – a small-time community access program that nobody watched. Because she did still have pages of notes left to talk about and she hadn't had a chance to get to some of her better arguments. People had warned her that Declan Quail of the *Declan Quail Show* wasn't going to let her get a word in edgewise. He seemed to have an inflated sense of import-ance about his opinions and his program. The very same people had told her that *no one* ever watched the *Declan Quail Show*.

Still, she'd maybe get a chance to state her busi-ness without sounding like a fool. And Quail's obscurity certainly didn't stop Sarah and Joanie from endlessly coaching her. Joanie had brushed Helen's brown locks until they shone and put some sort of product combin-ation in them that made them resemble, in shape and texture, some particularly expensive vertical blinds. Joanie had also assembled an outfit for her, out of scraps of her, Helen's, and Sarah's wardrobes. She employed the costume department of her experimental theater group, which consisted of two racks of wispy scarves, some top hats, tutus, several boxes of eyeglasses, costume jewelry, and a pixyish dresser named Madge. Joanie and Madge decided to give Helen clip-on earrings and a chunky necklace, which Joanie insisted brought out gold flecks in Helen's eyes. Helen couldn't see it. Her eyes were brown. She had always liked them, and she didn't think people needed to embellish in order to find them pretty. The dresser also insisted that Helen wear some sort of suit that seemed a size too small: Joanie told her it was sexier that way. She made up Helen's face and told her to sit still and not use her hands, arms, and torso.

It was very hard for her to keep her hands still.

She felt like some Robo-Avenging Angel, given how stiffly she was supposed to move and how much hardware was clanking around her. She wondered how she'd managed to endure all those heavily costumed and made-up dance performances she'd participated in as a teen. She had been used to all of this paraphernalia at some point in her life, wearing strange shoes, having her hair held viciously in place with hairspray and a million steely pins. Maybe that's what made it worse: She'd done it, she'd broken free of it, and she didn't want to go back. She had left that life, and she was glad of it. Now she wore what she wanted, ate what she wanted, and left her hair alone. And yes, it had been hard getting used to those freedoms – she still wasn't sure she was used to it – but it was harder reconciling herself to the restrictions she felt tonight.

So she sat in the tiny dressing room, fiddling with the necklace. Her hands needed something to do. Out of habit, she'd made patting motions at her hair, but withdrew without actually touching it. Joanie would probably kill Helen if anything happened to The Hair. (Although, she wasn't sure if she could alter it even if she tried.) Joanie was also the only person who knew the secret to removing whatever had been done to it. Maybe some sort of turpentine or solvent was involved. She wondered briefly what would happen if her hair stayed like this for the rest of her life. Would it set off metal detectors?

Oh, she was not nervous.

She rehearsed what she would say. She would go through the effects of multiple impacts on the brain. She would talk about how the brains of players looked on CT scans and how they looked at autopsy. She would describe tissue riddled with Lewy bodies and how that resembled the brains of Parkinson's patients. She would use examples. She would not venture opinions about stadiums, taxes, Russian billionaire NHL owners, or the Wolves hockey team and whether or not members of said team should be employed. If asked, she would say that she loved hockey, just not its violence.

She would be stupendously boring – correction – she would be droning, monotonous Robo-Avenging Angel with a shield of imperturbable hair, stunning opponents into sleep by extolling facts about the brain. No mutant hero had ever been quite like her. None could possibly follow.

There was a movement behind her. She looked up, way up, in the mirror, and her dreams of superhuman prowess fell to a gibbering death.

Adam Magnus. In a suit. And a scarf – a *jazzy* scarf.

His blue shirt brought out his eyes. Joanie would have admired his skill at wearing clothes. Helen preferred him without the clothing, but she could still appreciate this vision.

She swallowed hard.

"No one told me that you'd be here," Helen said.

A pause.

"No one told me you'd be here, either."

Well.

She looked down in her lap because looking back in the mirror meant looking at him.

She wasn't going to talk about his radio call, and she wasn't going apologize about the other night. Although now that she saw him in person, solid and gorgeous, she thought that maybe he deserved some sort of... something more. Not an explanation, either. It wasn't like she could even understand her own reasoning. The best she could do would be to put together a flowchart of her thought processes. They could bend their heads over it and study it together.

But for now, she should probably say something that struck the notes somewhere between lack of hard feelings, contrition, supreme indifference, and respect of their basic shared humanity. "Nice pinstripes."

It was the best she could come up with.

"Thanks. You look... uh, you look camera-ready," he said.

To her credit, she did not touch her coif or lick her rouged lips. She did, however, clench her fists.

Another encounter, another version of Helen. He had seen professional, white-coat-clad Helen. He had seen flirting Helen in the bar; naked, powerful, gorgeous Helen; and sad, vulnerable Helen. Now in the mirror, she looked immovable. Her folding chair was like a throne. Only her hands, white and tense, gave her away.

The hands made him want her.

He was probably in deep trouble again.

He held on to the back of her chair and let his fingers brush her back. She didn't flinch. He wasn't sure if this was good or bad.

"About the radio show thing, and the other night…"

"I was out of line that night. I'm sorry. But I'm still kinda mad at you about that NPR thing."

"Helen," he said.

Marin, the producer and camera operator, breezed in.

Helen turned around. "I wasn't told there'd be a debate. I feel ambushed."

"So do I," said Adam.

Marin smiled apologetically, as if that made up for it. "It's not a debate. It's more of a chance for each of you to say your piece, and if you want to respond, you both can."

"So it's a debate," Adam said, flatly.

Helen's mouth twisted. Whether she was trying to laugh, or whether she would cry, he didn't know.

–

"Welcome to the *Declan Quail Show*. I'm your host, Declan Quail, and today, we've got a segment we'd like to call 'Doc Versus Jock'."

Helen may have whimpered.

"As you know, the Oregon Wolves hockey team is no stranger to controversy. The new arena under construction by billionaire playboy Yevgeny Molotov, subsidized with taxpayer money to house the *pucksters*—" Quail paused to grin at the single camera "—has encountered significant resistance. But a new, hot controversy has arisen over whether hockey should even be played in Portland at all, and we at the *Declan Quail Show* have an *exclusive*. Our guests today are neurologist Helen Chang Frobisher, author of a recent piece calling for the end of the sport, and Adam Magnus, a defenseman for the Oregon Wolves hockey team."

They were seated in boxy chairs around a glass coffee table. It looked a little bit like the waiting room at the practice. Maybe it was supposed to give that sort of impression. But beyond the edges of their cramped space was a mess of wires, Marin, and two earnest interns. She took a deep breath. It was like an operating theater, she told herself, and she was the – not the surgeon, not the nurse, what? The anesthesiologist? Although, judging by the way Quail was still talking after the intro, she wouldn't be the one to put people to sleep.

She watched Quail's mouth open and close. His head was unusually large. It was probably good for TV.

She tried not to think of the fact that her left knee was suddenly itchy. She knew that it was just a trick of her nerves, but her hand wandered down to the hem of her skirt anyway.

Declan Quail seemed to be asking a question, but it was taking a long time to get to the meat of it. Plus, he was gazing into the camera instead of at his guests, so she wasn't sure to whom his query was addressed. She gave a surreptitious jab to the itchy spot and noticed that Adam was watching the movement.

His eyes strolled up to that spot, up her thighs. She felt a zing through her belly just as he reached that point.

This was not the time to remember Adam's hands playing at the hem of her green sweater that night. It was certainly not the time to recall the push of his body against her, and it was definitely not the time to shift in her chair.

She focused her attention back on Declan Quail. Miraculously, he was still talking.

"So Dr. Frobisher," he was saying, "are you saying that based on your extensive studies, this House of Hockey would be founded, as it were, on the blood of these young men's hopes and dreams? Are you saying that by building this structure, we are essentially dooming these athletes? Dr. Frobisher, I have one question for you: Do you think this arena should be built?"

Oh dear, it seemed that she had missed quite a lot.

"I don't know enough to comment on the arena," Helen said, as Declan Quail leaned toward her, hand on chin. "And it would probably not be up to code, you know, building an arena with blood."

She smiled weakly as she came to the end of that sentence. Declan Quail paused. She couldn't even look over at Adam. He was probably wincing at her terrible joke. *Fine!* she thought. *Let's see if you can do better.*

"But what I think," she said, raising her chin, "is that we need to concentrate on one issue here. Hockey leads to brain injury, and we need to prevent it. Lots of kids play it. Lots of them try to emulate hockey stars, who play hard because that's what is demanded of them from the sport. Maybe calling for a ban isn't helpful at all. Maybe we need to amend the way it's played."

"But from what I understand," Declan Quail said, "there are players whose function is simply to beat people up. *Enforcers*, they're called. Wouldn't you say that that would require a... a *sea change* on the ice?" He looked pleased with that. "And who are these so-called enforcers, really?"

"I'm one," Adam said, easily.

Despite her resolution, Helen caught his gaze full on. He quirked an eyebrow. He was enjoying this. Quail also switched directions and moved closer to him.

"Fighting is a part of the game. It's even sort of codified, if that makes sense. It's funny to say it, but there are internal rules about how and when the altercations take place. So yes, I've punched people, I've drawn blood. But there are limits to how even we enforcers are supposed to do it. Dr. Frobisher shows a lack of understanding about just how the game works. It's like using a sledgehammer to operate on a spine." He turned to Helen. "You know, to use metaphors you might be familiar with."

She almost stuck her tongue out at him. He said, "But it's also changing. The NHL—"

Quail interrupted here. "NHL?"

"The National Hockey League. The NHL has developed protocols, education, and policies in response to the danger of concussion. The sport is evolving. More pertinent to Portland, though, is the fact that this team hasn't had a chance to prove itself, and we can't if we aren't given room to grow."

"Do they deserve a chance, though? And at what price? Several million taxpayer dollars paid over to a playboy billionaire Russian?" He paused and glowered at the camera. "We'll be back after the break."

As soon as the light went off, all three of them slumped in their seats. "Thanks, good work so far," Quail muttered. He closed his eyes.

Helen began to tug at the microphone. "What are you doing?" whispered Adam.

"I am trying to leave," she said, not looking at him. "I should never have agreed to this. I'm done. I'm tired." She stopped pulling and let her hands drop. "I said I changed my mind about the issue on air. I don't care either way about the arena, and I wish you didn't have a job that gets you beat up, but I have no right to tell you what to do even though I want to all the time. I don't think anyone's paying attention to my crackpot editorial except our friends and a few anti-arena people trying to make this a story, so hopefully there's limited damage. But you were right. It's personal. I was wrong. I hurt you and I'm sorry. It was personal all along."

"Helen," he said.

"When you're a doctor, people tell you to be objective. I have never been good at that and I don't know why I thought I was with you. I'm not usually such a hothead. You're supposed to be the fiery one, the one who gets into fights. But instead, you're so… so *reasonable*."

"What every man longs to hear about himself. *Adam, you're a hyena in the sack and you're so, so… reasonable.*"

She laughed, a short, soft bleat that sounded forlorn, even to her.

He seemed to be about to say something, but one of the interns had come up and was fussing with the microphone that Helen had halfheartedly tried to remove.

The countdown began again, and Quail sat up abruptly, as if he'd swallowed an elixir that reanimated his corpse. He smiled at the camera. "Hello and welcome back to the *Declan Quail Show*. I'm your host, Declan Quail."

Chapter Ten

"Let me walk you to your car," Adam said.

The show was over. Quail had shaken hands and gone to scrub off his makeup. Martin offered them more water and made a threat to have them on again. Now it was just Adam and Helen and two interns rushing back and forth to clean up and leave.

The last thing Helen wanted to do was talk. She had just spent the last forever yakking away. But Adam had splayed his hand on the small of her back and was guiding her through the hallway and out the door. And she just wanted to lean back into him and enjoy it. But, of course, she couldn't.

The air was cool and fresh, and Helen breathed it in deeply and gratefully. She noticed that Adam did the same.

Now that it was over, she felt strange and hollow, as if she'd pushed herself to the edge of something important but that nothing in particular had happened. Nothing except that maybe instead of relaxing the way Joanie had coached her, Helen had stiffened progressively until she resembled her own shiny and shellacked TV hair.

Joanie would be disappointed.

Helen was going to have to get used to a lifetime of disappointing Joanie.

Adam had pulled a dark knit hat over his head. His coat, she noted when her hand brushed him briefly, was soft wool. She paused just outside the door of the television studio and frowned as she tried to remember where she had parked her car.

His hand dropped. "I'd feel better if you let me go with you," he said.

"Yes, I would, too. I…" She laughed nervously. "I just need a minute."

His presence wasn't helping her. It wasn't that she was dying of lust. But she suddenly wanted to give him something, something that would have him remember her. She would probably never see him again after this.

Then again, she'd had that thought before – a few times, at least.

She decided on a direction, and they set out across the parking lot. He hadn't tried to touch her again or speak to her. And despite her yearning to do something, she did not reach out, either.

After a somewhat roundabout walk, which was partly due to the fact that Helen was usually absentminded about these things, and partly due to the fact that she found Adam's presence distracting, they arrived in front of her car. It took another few minutes for her to find her car keys.

"I'm curious," he said, holding the door open for her.

He had good manners, she thought again. He had sung in a choir. He beat people up, and his forehead was still scarred. Nothing about him made sense to her. Nothing about her reaction to him made sense.

"Why this, Helen? And don't put me off with talk about your duty as a doctor. Something about this makes you afraid."

"Like I said in front of a camera and two interns who were pretending to mind their own business, I care about what happens to you."

He laughed shortly and pushed his hands through his hair. "No, we both know that's not it – or at least, it's not the only thing."

She had hurt his feelings, she could tell by the flex of his jaw, the downturn of his mouth. Her answer had been too quick, too flippant. And he, the big man, was trying to cover it up.

She could be brusque. She could tell him the interview was over, the cameras were off. She wanted to touch his shoulder, his cheek, run her finger along the bump on his nose. But it would hurt him more to pretend that they were to be that way with each other. It would never work.

Honesty. That was what she owed him.

"Get in the car," she said.

He was too big for her old Honda. He slid down immediately to try to make himself smaller, to make it seem like he wouldn't burst out of the roof, shoulders first. He was often trying to make himself look smaller, she realized, except on the ice. It was probably nice to have one place where he wouldn't have to try to make himself less – even if that place was a cold rink full of hostile men with sticks.

She swallowed.

"My father," she began. Unexpectedly, tears welled up and she was mortified. "My dad doesn't like sports," she whispered. She turned toward the window so that he wouldn't see. "I mean, not the way most people like sports. He didn't golf; he barely tolerated my brother's hockey games. He was doctor. Like me. I didn't think he even knew anything about sports, aside from the injuries that you could get from it. He had this thing about trampolines, I remember. Hated them. Thought they should be banned. Like father like daughter, I guess."

Adam laughed softly, and it made Helen feel a little calmer.

"But I remember watching the opening ceremonies of the Atlanta Olympics. I thought he was reading or maybe eating dinner, or something, I don't know. But when it came time to light the torch, I remember that they brought out the boxer, the former heavyweight champion of the world, Muhammad Ali. And beside me, I heard my dad breathe in this awed voice, *Cassius Clay.* It was... striking to hear my dad say that, for him to know that. I'd never heard him speak that way about anyone. I don't even know how to describe it to you. But at some point, he had followed boxing. At some point, he had watched Ali before he changed his name from Cassius Clay, and clearly, my dad had idolized the man when he was a kid, when he was the age that I was. It was like I had discovered something completely different about my father, like there was something clandestine that he had kept from us. It was like he'd announced he had a secret second family or something. Or maybe, it was the first time that I figured out that my dad had a whole life that didn't involve me. That he was a person. And worse, that cherished memory of Muhammad Ali was now... well, the man had become frail."

"I think I remember that," Adam said. "Ali was shaking as he lit the torch. His limbs, his face. He has Parkinson's or a form of it. It was..." He hesitated. "Maybe brought on by all those hits he took, right?"

"Parkinsonism," said Helen, distantly. "Atypical Parkinson's. And who knows if it was because of the boxing or a car accident, or anything. Some people take hard hits and are fine. Some take a few low-impact ones and develop CTE. But you can't prove anything unless you perform an autopsy. And even then... There's this vast middle stretch when someone is alive, when the body is there and it is failing and the mind is locked in, becoming frailer. And you don't know what to do – there's nothing you can do to stop it. You can only watch."

A pause. "So not only was I discovering something about my dad that I'd never imagined, I was watching something that had maybe crushed him, changed his worldview. He really grieved to see Ali – Cassius Clay – in that condition. And I, well, I found that that opened up the door to ask questions about other parts of his life, his past. It turned out he was a boxer when he was younger. I should have seen it, probably, the scars, the broken nose.

I never really questioned him before that point. And then I had a lot of other questions after that, not just about sports but also about how strange we were – how strange our family seemed compared to everyone else. I never thought of the fact that even though my dad's parents – my grandparents – lived in the same small town, we never really saw them or talked about them or that it was because they were upset that he'd married my mom, who is of Chinese descent. There's so much I don't know about what happened to my dad, and the worst is not knowing what gave him this disease or knowing what to do about it. I've turned it over in my head so often, and I suspect it was a series of minor hits over the years from boxing, from accidents. But it could have been stress, or genetics could play a part, too. I'll never know for sure, and that kills me."

–

Adam saw her tears in the reflection of the window. He resisted reaching for her.

"My dad's disease makes him go in and out," she said. "Maybe that's worse because it makes me think that something will just click back into place and he will be back. Sometimes, we're on the telephone and he'll be asking me about my practice, how many patients I see, how old most of them are, what do they do. We'll have a professional conversation. And then I'll forget. I'll start asking him for advice on something or another, how to handle a difficult patient, what to do when someone gets too personal, how

I should talk to someone's family, and I'll realize that he's hung up the phone or he's simply left it or he's dropped it. That he has lost control of his muscles and can't move his jaw or his tongue. I've forgotten that he can't do things. That's almost cruel. And the worst thing is, I know. I'm a doctor. I know exactly what this is, what this is going to be, and still, I forget."

He did touch her this time, once, his fingers to her elbow.

"He was always there when I needed him," she said. "That's such a cliché. It's not even accurate – he was busy. But he always had a solution to problems, some that hadn't even been formulated. He thought about the things that I told him. When I went away to school, he'd send me notes that he'd written in the middle of the night when everyone else was asleep, just things that occurred to him that he hadn't told me before then. He had pretty good handwriting and very bad eating habits. He wrote on a lot of fast food napkins. I wish I'd saved them. I never thought I'd have to."

She heaved in another breath.

"And the funny thing is, I'm just like him. I eat Pop-Tarts and popcorn, and I know what's good for me, and I don't do anything about it. The one concession he had to health was that he wouldn't eat toast."

"Pop-Tarts yes, toast no."

"He said it was carcinogenic. He and my mother had battles over the toaster. She set it on high, and he barely tolerated warm bread. He loved barbecue, though. Completely illogical, I know."

137

She looked at him. Her tone was almost conversational now. "I'm not logical, you know. I try and try, and then I fail spectacularly."

They were quiet for a while. It was dark now, and he couldn't really see her face, except in the reflection in the window.

"He had a few accidents. And then, it was like something came loose. The onset of disease was rapid," she said, finally. "Well, that's not true. It had been happening for years, but no one noticed. Well, he would have noticed, if it had been his own patient. But I... didn't."

She tried to laugh, but it came out as a strangled cry. The sound shot straight to his heart. "I'm trying to explain," she said. "But I'm making a muddle of it."

He shushed her. She was staring straight ahead now, and he sensed that she didn't want him to look at her anymore.

"So, I guess this is good-bye," she said.

No, he thought.

But that was impractical – *they* were all wrong for each other. She was frail. He was... not much better. Instead, he nodded. He'd been telling himself that since the beginning. It was better for both of them.

"For the record," she said, "I think you're... well, I wish things had been different. I wish *I* had been different."

"I wish I were different, too," he said.

He squeezed her hand and got out of the car.

Chapter Eleven

"You're wanted upstairs," Brooks the GM said, avoiding Adam's eyes.

Well, the moment had finally come. He was going to be fired.

He had imagined it would take place after a particularly bad game. But they'd won another last night. He'd even scored a goal, and the crowd – yes, there had been a slightly larger crowd – had cheered for him. It had felt pretty good. Not the best thing ever, but not bad.

In any case, best to go out on top – or as near the top as he would ever get.

He unlaced his skates and began to pull off his jersey. Brooks said, "I mean *now*."

"At least let me put on a pair of shoes or something," Adam said irritably.

Brooks looked nervous and he began to pace.

For pity's sake.

Adam sighed. "Fine."

He did pause to at least put on some sneakers, but he was a mess. "Aren't you coming with me?" he asked Brooks.

But the man was already gone. Coward.

When Adam entered the meeting room, he frowned. There wasn't a familiar face among them. And they were all men – except for one young African American woman. She was also the only one to smile at him, so he looked away, and his gaze landed on someone whose face was a little more familiar.

Yevgeny Molotov.

Adam's billionaire boss, his papers, and his devices took up the long side of a rectangular table. Everyone else was crammed around the remaining sides. The man made a gesture, inviting Adam to sit, but there were no chairs. Adam preferred to stand anyway, which forced Molotov to tip his head back a little. Off the ice, Adam didn't usually like his overgrown body, but today he didn't mind.

"You're finally here," Molotov said.

"Sorry to keep you waiting. I only heard about this meeting two minutes ago."

Molotov's handsome face looked faintly bored, faintly amused. He wore a suit, no tie. His shirt was open at the collar. He had that European litheness that came from cigarette smoking and vitamin-D deficiency.

Adam had met the man once, at some sort of party for the Wolves. He had a woman on each arm and another following him. Actually, probably several. Apparently, no woman could resist his money, and his accent, which drifted in and out, and his cold, gray eyes.

It was so cheesy.

Adam schooled his face into farm-boy stoicism and wiped the sweat with the bottom of his shirt.

He waited. Only fair. After all, he'd kept Molotov waiting for two whole minutes.

"Mr. Magnus," Molotov said, after a long silence. "That was an interesting game last night."

"Thanks."

"I saw clips from the interview you gave the other night, defending hockey in Portland. Under the terms of your contract, of course, you're supposed to be checking with us before making public appearances, even if it is on a small-town TV program."

Adam's stomach clenched. It was true; he hadn't exactly run his appearances by Wolves central command. But who listened to public radio? Who watched that clown, Declan Quail? No one ever watched Declan Quail.

"Janel here tells me that you were found… acceptable by the people who did watch that little program the other day. We need a recognizable face, one that is a little different from my own. We'd like you to step up your appearances, but of course we would have to have Janel here groom you."

Molotov's tone implied that Adam would need a lot of grooming.

The woman who Adam assumed was Janel intervened at this point. "We've faced an unusual amount of resistance, trying to get this arena project built. It would be good if we could give the team a face and a voice in these last months before the vote goes before state legislators. Someone to remind them that they want this."

"That's a little more the team captain's job, isn't it?"

"Yes, but as Yevgeny noted, a few key people are beginning to pay attention to you thanks to your writing and your debate. You have a certain chemistry with Dr. Frobisher, too. The redirection, shall we say, has served us twofold: First, it can be used as an excellent diversionary tactic, away from the question of arena funding and into more academic questions about the morality of sport et cetera, et cetera. No one's really likely to win that one. Second, attendance has gone up, and interest has gone up – perhaps because of the win or possibly because more people are paying attention to you than previously suspected. The numbers are pretty modest, but we've done a little testing and apparently Portlanders like that sort of stoic, sensible modesty that you project. We could also offer you a bonus for the extra work that you'd put in."

Adam thought quickly. "What kind of bonus?"

"Thirty thousand."

Adam couldn't help noticing that Molotov looked bored.

Must be nice.

But it was a good thing they'd bypassed Adam's manager, Bobby, and come directly to Adam to negotiate. Bobby would have jumped on the offer right away.

"I'd be happy to help out. But… I wonder if in addition to the bonus, Janel would be interested in teaching me more about the business and operations side of the game."

Janel beamed approvingly. "Looking to the future," Janel said. "I think that's a great idea. Molotov Interna-

142

tional has a lot of opportunities in operations. At the very least, we can give you some good fundamentals in PR."

Molotov flicked a speck of dust from his sleeve. "We'll have to test him over the course of a few more appearances."

"Of course, sir," Janel said.

They turned to each other and began talking in hushed tones.

Adam realized he'd been dismissed.

He gave a halfhearted wave at them and trudged back down to change. *What the hell just happened?*

Apparently, he'd gained the possibility of a new job? Of course, if he had to work more with Molotov, he'd probably end up punching the guy. But Janel seemed fine. Besides, he thought, looking down at his filthy jersey, he really wasn't in a position to refuse.

–

"I'd like to talk to you about your recent forays into the media, Dr. Frobisher," Dr. Weber said, intercepting her before she left.

Well, it was about time that she was called to the carpet, or the linoleum, or whatever it was that lined the hospital hallway.

Helen's shift was over. She had been keeping her head down, hoping to escape and go home and brood. Unfortunately, she was wearing her green and orange bike leggings. No one ever even came close to hitting her on the road, although she was sure that her bright gear had caused many accidents. Most likely, it was from people swerving to get away from the awful tie-dye. It figured that on the day that she'd hoped to make her way home quietly, she'd (1) brought the wrong wardrobe and (2) run into the hospital's hockey fanatic.

No one ever watches Declan Quail, my ass, she thought as Dr. Weber pointed her outside to the small garden adjacent to the hospital. It was a cold day, and no one was outside. *No one to hear me scream*, Helen thought irrationally. Weber would drown her in the koi pond for going after his team. He was way too nice for anyone to suspect he was capable of foul play. *She* wouldn't even suspect him, even if he held her under the swampy water. He'd probably manage to convince her that she was helping him look for his eyeglasses.

It was the perfect crime. No one would miss her. She did regret that she was going to die in these stupid leggings, though.

She hadn't exactly cleared her escapades with the hospital's PR department. Well, it was Dr. Weber's fault that she even knew of the Wolves' existence. Although, to tell the truth, revenge and yelling weren't Weber's style.

"So, you're on a one-woman campaign to rid Portland of hockey."

"Well, I'm hardly alone. Although, I guess my motives are a little different." She added, "I wasn't speaking for the hospital. I made that clear."

"Yes, you made it clear. And no, you weren't speaking for the hospital."

Weber smiled. Helen shifted uneasily.

"You're not in trouble, Dr. Frobisher, and to tell you the truth, I hadn't heard about it until Aditi, our social media manager, brought it up. She has a news alert set up for the hospital, I guess. In any case, we're having our annual charity softball game to raise money for the new children's wing. I wondered if you'd play. Chair of the board Dr. Mimi Chister is particularly interested in your participation. And so am I."

Well, that was the last thing she'd been expecting.

"We call it the SnowBall game, even though we don't get snow here. Just a little joke. Usually, the orthopedic surgeons and cardiologists sign up for all the spots. But we wanted to change it up a little this year. Not so much that we lose, mind, but you're clearly an athletic young woman. You'd *fit* right in."

He twinkled at his pun. The leggings were a joke, she wanted to yell. Because she'd concentrated so much on dance, she hadn't really used bats or nets or cleats or sticks or any of the equipment associated with fitness.

"I'm not great at team sports," she said.

He waved his hand dismissively. "Board chair specifically asked me to ask you," said Weber. "You might know about her. Her husband is a developer. They've got an ax to grind with the new arena, too. Besides, we're hoping we can make it into a bit of a grudge match. Some publicity for either side won't hurt. Adam Magnus is on the opposing team. And there'd be a brief radio spot."

Oh.

No.

She got up. "It's been nice. Thank you so much for the offer to play t-ball—"

"Softball."

"Whatever. But no. I am not being pitted against Adam Magnus again—"

Weber was going to interrupt, but she held up her hand.

"In a venue that is sure to be even more personally humiliating than public radio or the *Declan Quail Show*."

Or my car, she added silently.

She had planned to never see the man again. He'd held her hand and she'd liked it, for God's sake. Was she in grade three? She felt ashamed of herself. Why, oh why, did the universe want to humiliate her?

"Listen, Helen," Weber said, smiling, "You're young. You're photogenic. And you're the closest thing that this hospital has to a public figure right now."

"Two appearances on local shows that no one watches or listens to? That's pathetic. What about that nurse who wrote medical thrillers? She's got to be more famous than me."

"She moved to Seattle for a new post last month. Don't worry, you're going to help us raise money. A little ball playing, some publicity stuff. Maybe you'll judge the organic apple pie eating contest or whatever the planning committee usually does. The first practice is tomorrow at six. Everybody's busy with the holidays and such, but we've all cleared our schedules. I'll make sure you're on the e-mail list. Did I mention I'm the coach?"

Yelling wasn't Weber's style, Helen decided, but revenge definitely was.

–

What choices did he have? He had gone to a career counselor and taken more tests. He filled out a stack of application packages from colleges, but he suspected that it was probably just a make-work project for himself.

Molotov was rich and powerful, and he could make things happen anywhere. Plus, it wasn't good to antagonize him. There were rumors on the team that their last center was flipping burgers at a downtown diner. Although all the "diners" in downtown Portland seemed pretty upscale and weren't likely to hire an inexperienced ex-hockey player for the kitchens, truth be told. The rumor mill at Wolf lair was not known for its accuracy.

He had told Molotov and Janel that yes, he'd give the PR stints a try. Janel, it turned out, was the head of Molotov corporate's PR on the West Coast. Rumor had it that she was one of Molotov's ex-girlfriends, but Adam couldn't see it. She seemed too sharp and too upbeat to have ever once been with Molotov. She was a quick worker and very thorough. Janel soon had a new schedule for Adam. She took out file pictures they had of him and went through his wardrobe and loaded his smartphone with suit, jacket, and tie combinations for future appearances. She said he could stand to go a little more casual. She was a toucher, too. In fact, she had her fingers on his shoulder now, in the cafeteria in the Wolves' training facility. They were going over his schedule.

He could always beg to go back to the farm, he thought as he shrugged out of Janel's insistent grip.

Truth was, he wasn't needed. Farming was a hard life, and most years, his sister, Jennifer, and her family just scraped by. They wouldn't be able to make room for him. When he was young, he had hauled a lot of hay and cleaned a lot of manure out of barns. He was the first in his family to go to college; his brother, Jim, was the second.

He saw his parents, his siblings, and his nephews at Christmas and when he went to Minnesota to play. When he signed with his first team, someone put a banner over Main Street that read, "Home of Adam Magnus." He heard that it had blown down in a storm after the first week and brought a tree down with it. No one bothered replacing it.

His family didn't know much but they could probably trace his emotional health through the ups and downs in his stats. Hell, he hardly knew exactly what had happened. His drinking had started in the first year after being drafted and had gotten worse when he'd been kicked down to the minors. His memory of those years was fragmented: beeriness and vomit, terrible keyboard music, forgetting how to lace up his skates, a strip club in Utah where the dancers hadn't been allowed to peel down beyond their skivvies. He started wearing his hair short then as a way of ensuring that he would not wake up with puke in his hair – or with a mullet. There had been fights. Most of them had taken place off the ice.

He'd pulled it together eventually and fought his way back to the majors, but a part of him wondered if it was too late for his poor abused brain. If Helen Frobisher were to aim a flashlight into his skull, would his gray matter be riddled with darker pockets? Would she be disgusted with him? Appalled? Would she pity him? Would she hold his hand?

He doubted that she'd hold his hand.

The crush he had on her – that he still had on her, after all of this – was just entirely too pathetic.

He took a sip of his coffee, and Janel finally took her hand off his shoulder to tap on her iPhone. She gave him a wide smile. *I'm listening*, her eyes said, even though she wasn't. She was checking her messages.

With that, she stood up. He half rose, too. "I'll see you tonight, then," she said, and tried to pat him on the head.

He winced away. If she noticed, she didn't show it. Some people were good at that – selective noticing.

"Who's that?" Serge asked, sliding in place.

Adam looked at his friend's tray. "New minder."

Serge squinted at the retreating heels. "I wouldn't mind being minded by her."

Serge picked up a plastic fork and shoved it unenthusiastically into a fruit salad. "Everyone was speculating about your little meeting with Yevgeny today. You agreed to be the team's spokesmonkey?"

"That's what everyone's saying?"

Serge frowned at a grape that he had speared. He released it gently on his tray. "Throws you against the lovely Helen Frobisher for a while, doesn't it?"

"I think the phrase is *throws me in with*."

"I'm French."

"French *Canadian*. Your English is great. You said it that way on purpose."

Or maybe Adam's imagination was in hyperdrive if one little word choice was enough to drive him crazy.

Serge pursed his lips and deposited another unsatisfactory piece of fruit on his tray. "Will you stop that?" Adam said. "The cantaloupe is fine. That grape is fine. *I am fine*. This is a good opportunity for me to get into something new and different. Who knows, maybe I can make a career out of it."

"Hockey punditry?"

"Hockey commentary. Local hockey commentary. Okay, very local, so far. But Yevgeny has interests all over the world."

Serge shook his head. "You don't want to do that. It's a short life. You have to make quips. You have to suck up and analyze. You don't even like hockey that much anymore. Your whole life will be tied to talking about it."

"Or maybe I can be seen as management material."

"You aren't enough of an asshole douche nozzle to be management material."

"Like I said, your English is *great*."

"You're Adam Magnus, the mild-mannered metalhead, not micromanaging moron Magnus."

"I wear suits. I like suits."

"You wear them too well. If you want to be in management, you should have expensive clothing that is poorly tailored. It shows you don't have enough time for alterations. All you care about is work."

The goalie sounded petulant.

"Serge, why don't you want me to change? Do you have a problem with this stuff? Do you have a problem with me?"

Serge pushed his tray away and stood up.

"Yeah, of course I do. What do you expect? I see you making plans. You can't wait to go. Well, where does that leave me?"

"You already have plans, Serge. Remember? The family restaurant?"

"I hate those plans," Serge said.

He picked up his fruit salad, replaced the lid, and tossed it into the garbage container. It was a beautiful shot.

Serge started to walk away, then he paused. Without looking, he said, "All I ever wanted to do was play hockey. It's all I want to do. You're not even really here anymore, Adam. You're already gone."

Chapter Twelve

SNOWBALL GAMES: DOCS VS. JOCKS, the posters screamed. Apparently, this phrase was a thing now. For the seven thousandth time, Helen muttered something about how apparently people *did* actually watch the *Declan Quail Show* despite the fact that no one admitted to it.

It was the day after Thanksgiving – American Thanksgiving, as Helen still thought of it, even after all these years – and another practice had been called. Weber had not lied. Most of the players were orthopedic surgeons, male, and they had their own game shorthand. Or maybe they were just jerks. During practice, Helen had been exiled to some obscure spot in the outfield where she stood staring at the clouds. She didn't really mind. She could hang out in the cold, mushy field, not really having to think or pay attention to anything for long periods of time. Or rather, she thought she didn't have to pay much attention. When they left the field, they had to call her repeatedly before, finally, Dr. Al McGinnis came out and escorted her back. He didn't respect her softball skills or her as a person, clearly, but that didn't stop him from making a pass at her. With a swish of her hair and a well-aimed smile, she could probably have a date, she thought, trudging through the mud. She squelched through the field as sloppily as she could and frowned discouragingly.

She wasn't uncoordinated or weak, she thought defensively as Al McGinnis explained the finer points of the game to her. Actually, they weren't finer points. He seemed to think that she needed to learn the basic rules. She could understand basic rules, as if Weber – and really, life in North America – hadn't already taken care of that. She hit the ball decently once or twice. It was hard to tell if she could catch, because no one threw to her, and certainly, no one let anything anywhere near her.

Al McGinnis was probably the kind of person she should date. They were both doctors, so they would have things to talk about. Except, she didn't care about anything he said. Now he seemed to be talking about some sort of knee replacement surgery he was trying to perfect.

She said something about an anterior cruciate ligament injury she'd suffered, and he said, "Dancer, right?"

"Former."

"I can tell by the way you move. You've got the build."

He probably thought that was a great line, too. Adam had said something similar to her once. But he'd said it better.

She considered Al McGinnis's lips. They were fine. Nice, even. His hair was sandy; he had a good tan. Tall. Meaty hands.

Ugh.

He was adequate. If she could date people like him, maybe she would forget Adam. Maybe she'd have a life.

Maybe she'd stop worrying about her dad. Maybe she would be able to sleep through the night without running endlessly over things she'd said, things she'd failed to say, better drug combinations for her father, drug combinations to soothe herself.

Her dad would be out of hospital soon. He had a space in a nice place, according to her brother. Rosedale Senior Assisted Living Facility, it was called. It probably didn't have roses, and it likely wasn't in a dale. Her mom had already found an apartment nearby. They hadn't put the house on the market yet, and Helen felt a hard knot of happiness about the fact that it was still theirs. It was immature and it didn't help her family, but the knowledge that the wide porch was still there with the stained crocheted rug and that the town was there, unchanging, had been the only thing that kept her sane sometimes, especially in those hard days when she had been at the ballet school.

"We should come up with Roller Derby names," said Helen brightly, interrupting whatever Al McGinnis was talking about. "We'll strike fear into the hearts of our opponents. I can be Hell-On Wheels. Maybe I can be *Helen Killer.*"

"This isn't Roller Derby."

Her team was no fun.

The game was scheduled for the next day. She wished for rain, and in the grand scheme of things, it wasn't that big a demand; she did, after all, live in Portland. When the clouds persisted, she thought that maybe her modest prayers had been answered. But it was not to be. The field fogged up, little droplets came close to coalescing into big ones, but rain did not come to pass.

The gods hated her.

She put on the garish pink team jersey. It was a little big. No one else on her bro-boy team had a jersey in this particular color. They also managed to get her a gigantic pink baseball hat. She liked pink but this was annoying. To complete the hideousness of her outfit, she decided to wear the tiger-striped tights, despite the fact that she'd be ridiculed. She was going to be ridiculed for her playing anyway. Why not just go all the way? If she could find a clown nose, she would have donned it.

Part of her understood that she would be seeing Adam again and not under great circumstances. Then again, when had they ever been really good? She had first met him after he was in an accident. Then, she'd run into him on the street and yelled at him (which still managed to lead to sex). Then he had been angry with her after the editorial, and he'd called in for that disastrous radio show. Then there was the last time, during that stupid TV appearance.

She told herself that he'd listened to her that night after the *Declan Quail Show* out of pity, that she felt ashamed of herself for breaking down that way, that she had said too much and felt too much. But she couldn't muster up the proper defiance. Something about him crept behind her defenses. Maybe it was his strength and solidness, not in body, but in spirit. Despite his aggression on the ice, in person he was overwhelmingly gentle. His big fingers whispered across her skin like a loving ghost.

She frowned at her reflection and told herself it didn't matter what she looked like. In fact, this was great, perfect. It inspired just the right amount of repulsion. He would not want to touch her while she looked like this. She should smudge dirt under her eyes – or whatever it was that ballplayers painted their faces with – to complete the picture.

She should probably be psyching herself up for the game instead of reverse primping.

She gave one last look to the mirror. "Do your best," she said, "or do your worst."

The bleachers were crowded that day. Helen liked to think it was because there were a lot of people who wanted a renovated children's wing, but she knew that the hospital publicity machine had been working overtime to make this a grudge match. It was probably nice to be in the stands, to know which side to root for, to expect a clear score.

Chairwoman Chister approached her and introduced herself. She was slim and beautiful, and her bob was so sharp it would have sliced Anna Wintour to shreds. The chair introduced her husband, the developer. There was a flash as someone took a picture of Helen and Chairwoman Chister's anti-arena developer husband shaking hands.

She should have known there would be pictures. She was clad in tiger-striped leggings, an oversize pink jersey, and an ugly baseball cap, and she looked a movie producer's idea of a feisty-but-lovable grand-mother, dressed for a rousing game of bingo.

The husband just winked at her. Chister's husband was a winker.

She saw the celebrity athletes from the other team approaching. They had not bothered with matching uniforms, probably because they knew that everyone would take one look at them and know who they were. Well, everyone except for her. Too bad they hadn't asked anyone from the ballet to join them.

The rest of the doc team was beaming. They were excited to meet their adversaries.

She scowled and caught sight of Adam. He raised an eyebrow and mock-frowned at her. She pulled her cap lower over her head as if she thought the pink would camouflage her and hung back, but he sidled right up to her and put his big warm hand on her back, and she felt her insides turn into hot fudge sauce. She increased the fierceness of her glower, but didn't step away.

"They're going to want a picture," she growled.

"Are you worried that you're going to outshine me?" he asked, pulling her cap up so that he could look into her eyes. "That's very kind of you."

"Oh, shut up," she said.

"Nice hat," he said. "Why is yours pink?"

"It matches my vagina," she said, sourly.

He quirked a smile. "Not quite," he said, in her ear.

She flushed so warmly that her heels tingled. "Right. Now the hat just matches my face."

"And why is the shirt so big?" he asked.

"All the better to house my enormous rippling muscles. At least, that's what my teammates probably thought when they ordered it."

"I'm surprised you agreed to play," he said.

"I didn't exactly jump at the chance to be the team mascot. But here I am."

"At least they didn't dress you up like a mallard or an adorable little wolf. Actually, I don't think I'd mind seeing you in a wolf costume."

It was her turn to whisper in his ear. "Were you always this dirty?"

—

She would probably look good in his jersey, he thought, imagining the shiny drape of the material over her chest, the hem just skimming the curve of her ass. If he were being realistic, the shirt would probably hit her much lower. Then again, how realistic was it to picture her smiling at him that way again? And how realistic was it to imagine that she would be slowly taking that item of clothing off and tossing it to the side?

She *was* blushing, though.

He *really* shouldn't think of her this way right now, he realized, as his own body tightened. Especially when she was so close that he could smell her. He didn't understand how ballplayers could walk around in these little sweats. He coughed, and she looked at him quizzically.

"I'm glad I caught you two together!" a man said, inserting himself between the two of them.

They both jumped back a little guiltily, which was silly because they were in full view of the field. Then again, they had been talking about her vagina.

"Dr. Frobisher, I'm Karl Pallas, a producer for KPOT Sports Radio. You and Adam here—" the stranger clapped Adam's back, "are going to chat about hockey a little, maybe talk a little trash. All PG, radio friendly of course."

"Well of course. It's for charity," Helen said.

Adam could tell she was talking between gritted teeth. As the producer fiddled with his recorder, Helen's hands opened and shut, as if she wanted to rip the equipment out of the guy's hands or dig a hole deep in the earth and drop down into the ground. He wouldn't mind joining her. Except that Janel was not five feet away now, pretending not to hover. He smiled brightly, even though this was radio.

"I tell you, this arena and the brain injury thing are the most exciting things to happen to the Wolves all season," Karl was saying.

He held a huge mike in Helen's face expectantly. "Oh. You're recording. You want me to comment on that," Helen said.

Janel was probably snickering if she heard that, and Adam felt defensiveness on Helen's behalf rise up. She hadn't spent hours and hours in media training learning how to respond to nonquestions the way he had.

Plus, she was already starting to get riled. "Listen, I couldn't give a flying f— a flying fig about this arena. But I do care about the way people play this sport. I care about education and training. And I recognize that the NHL has taken steps to curb the risks. But watching it as a doctor – as a person who cares about what it can do to a body – it's just terrifying."

"But that's what people like," Karl said. "That's part of the appeal."

Helen threw up her hands, another gesture that was lost on the radio. Adam could tell it was all starting to get to her. But, of course, if she lost control in the media, it would be over. He tried to divert. "Hey, hey, I can't believe you think the arena's the best thing to happen to the Wolves. What about the last few games? We're working hard on offense over there, but Korhonen's really coming into his own."

Karl looked relieved to be talking about sports with a man. Helen rolled her eyes, but Karl didn't notice, so singular was his focus on Adam.

After a few more quips and shoulder pats, Karl turned dutifully back to Helen. "Bobby from Healy Heights wants to know why you're against fun."

Helen's mouth opened. She gave Karl a narrow-eyed look. Then she grabbed the mike from his hand. "That's right, Bobby, I'm against fun. I'm against being people being so punch drunk that they forget their kids' birthdays, names, how to stand, if they've eaten. I'm against fights and injuries that lead to a grown man being unable to bring a drink to his mouth because his arms are trembling so much he can't hold a cup without sloshing half the beer over himself. I'm against being people being so incapacitated that they choke on a mouthful of soup that someone has fed them. I'm against the kind of culture that doesn't want to change that because that's how the game is played. I do get to see what happens afterward, though. You may not agree with my thoughts. I'm not sure I know the best way either – maybe my statements are a blunt instrument. But I do know that I am firmly against this happening to people when it can be prevented. So yeah, I'm against fun, all right. Because apparently this kind of fun is completely fucking overrated."

She handed the mike back to Karl.

"I'm sorry I used an expletive on the air," she said.

Karl laughed nervously. "Thanks for talking to us," he said.

Helen leaned into the microphone. "You're welcome," she said very loudly and smiled at him as she walked away.

Karl almost seemed to apologize to Adam after Helen's outburst, and Adam felt an almost irrational desire to laugh his ass off. He couldn't summon up any annoyance with her – not anymore. He wrapped up his comments as quickly as he could and followed after Helen.

"Well, that was a terrible interview," she said, almost cheerfully as Adam caught up with her. "I seem to be getting worse and worse."

She made no move to get away from him. Even in her silly costume, she was compelling. The tiger tights should not have looked good on her, but the stripes delineated every firm curve of her legs. The hat, though, that bothered him.

"I think you broke all the PR rules in less than ten minutes," he said.

"And I really only spoke for one or two of those minutes," she said. "I like to be liked. I want people to like me. But this is important to me. So I guess I'm the downer asshole."

"Downer asshole in a terrible hat that hides your face. Your beautiful face."

He turned the cap backward on her head so that he could see her eyes. "Stop it," she said, turning it back. More softly, she said, "You're flirting with me."

She made a motion like she would walk away. He could swear that she was blushing. "We always flirt with each other," he said.

"Yes, but…"

Someone was calling for their attention. The game was about to begin. Helen went back to join her team.

He didn't pay attention to the introduction or the speech. The sandy-haired guy standing too close to Helen was a distraction. He was probably another doc. Adam wondered how well they knew each other. Helen wasn't that interested in Sandy, though. She kept her eyes hidden under the hat. One by one, a black-haired woman with a severe bob called out their names. There were no actual baseballers here today. Serge was here, and a few basketball players were huddled together. There was also a skateboarder and a former Olympic skier and a golfer. Helen, he noticed, got a wolf whistle from the stands. He thought he recognized Helen's friend, Petra.

It was nice to be able to look into the stands in the middle of a pleasant Saturday, he thought, with people cheering honestly and without rancor. The bobbed woman was calling his name, and he waved.

He received an unexpected roar, too. That felt kind of nice. The tips of his ears were probably pinkening.

The Jocks were up at bat. Golfer was up first.

It became clear fairly early on that the Docs took this far more seriously than the Jocks. Adam's team hadn't attempted to practice together. They had been introduced shortly before the game, and Adam figured they were supposed to rely on their natural athleticism to get them through the day. The Docs, meanwhile, had been stretching, clapping their hands to their chests in some sort of complicated handshake, and visualizing – with the exception of Helen. They engaged in some other physiologically tested exercises. It was kind of impressive. They probably had been pretty good players in high school. A few thought they could really take on a group of professional athletes. They certainly were dressed like a more cohesive team than the Jocks, right down to their surgeon-green uniforms – well, again with the exception of Helen.

Golfer walked up to plate with a five-iron in his hand. He waggled his bottom and stared down the pitcher. The crowd hooted. There was more unsubtle butt movement.

Adam wondered how Helen had been roped into it. He doubted that she had a Russian billionaire breathing

164

down her neck. Golfer finally picked up a real softball bat and swung mightily. The ball connected. He was on first.

The Docs were in trouble.

Helen, he noted, was doing a tree pose in short center field. She was trying to be subtle about it, but there it was. He smiled to himself. When she thought no one was looking, she pulled her leg back in another stretch.

Beside him, Serge laughed softly. "You're staring at her," he said.

"So what?" Adam muttered.

"So, to an objective outside observer, it looks like you're crazy about her. And it didn't help that you were glued to her side before. Also, Yevgeny's minion is glaring at you."

Janel *was* glaring, in between texting furiously.

"She should be happy with any kind of publicity," Adam murmured.

Serge shrugged. "I'm up," he said. "You can borrow my stick."

"Wait, what?"

Serge didn't answer. He pulled on his goalie mask and walked out onto the field. The crowd roared. Serge put his hands to his mask and blew kisses.

Adam looked at the hockey stick that Serge had left behind. *That's* what Serge thought he should bat with? He sighed. Well, at least he was good at hitting things.

By the sixth inning, the Jocks were up thirteen to three. The Docs were having constant conferences. They were determined to be serious – except for Helen. She had apparently given up any pretense of paying attention and was now doing a full-on yoga demo. She was her own show. Adam had given up any hope of doing anything besides staring and hoping that she would perform downward facing dog. At bat, she connected with the ball well enough, and she ran quickly, more swiftly than some of those lumbering docs who yelled and screamed at her to keep moving. *It's just a fucking game*, he wanted to yell at them. His fists clenched, and he heard Serge laughing all the way from home plate where he wore his goalie mask instead of catcher's gear.

Helen didn't let it bother her. She settled at first and did something crazy and incredible with her back leg. He watched and ground his teeth as a basketball player tried to chat her up. She gave him a sweet smile.

Adam felt tense. Maybe he needed to take up yoga.

Those hoping for some sort of midrun speech from Helen had given up quickly. Golfer had put on a pair of neon pink jodhpurs and was prancing around the outfield, clearly egging on the docs. In the stands, kids chomped on soy dogs. Adam had scored a run with his hockey stick, and caught a pop fly in his baseball cap. He felt like he had done his part.

And the Docs were out. At the seventh inning stretch, some kids, maybe a few of the healthier ones from the children's wing, did a choreographed number. In the middle of it, they grabbed some of the players to come up and dance with them. Track Star did a fancy break-dance move. The doctors had no sense of rhythm. Well, again, except for Helen. She wasn't doing anything difficult, but she moved in a way that was so carefree and yet joyful, it was so much better than all of them combined. She whipped her supple body around the spins and gave a flourish to her kicks.

She must have been incredible to watch at fifteen, sixteen, seventeen. Of course, she probably would never have given an ungainly, hormone-crazed guy like him the time of day. Not that she would now, not that he had, apparently, changed much. He would forever be catching up with her. A hearty cheer signaled the end of the routine.

If this were like any of the games they played when he was a kid, maybe the teams would go out for pizza afterward. The Docs looked like sore losers, though.

Maybe he could suggest going out for pizza.

And maybe he could get her alone in a corner booth and take her out to laser tag. And maybe they could neck in the backseat of his car.

God, what was he thinking?

But at that moment, the woman with a sharply cut bob stepped up to the plate with a microphone.

She introduced herself as the chair of the hospital and kept her remarks brief, thanking the attendees and the players. But the jolt came at her next words. "And now, here to judge the Snowball Tourney's Annual Exceptional Chicken Contest, Dr. Helen Frobisher and Oregon Wolves hockey player, Adam Magnus!"

An exceptional children contest – or was it an exceptional chicken contest? And he was the judge? What. The. Fuck.

He shot a look at Janel who waved him to the plate. He jogged up to it and joined Helen. Again.

"Just remember," the woman with the sharp bob murmured, leaning in to shake his hand, "it's all in fun."

Helen crouched down to shake the kids' hands, and Adam, knees protesting, did the same.

"What's your name?" Helen asked a young, redheaded girl.

"Lariat," the kid said. "And my chicken is a Silkie! Her name is Wilhelmina."

The next kid, Thoreau with his chicken, Zandra. And Stogie with Caramel.

"This is the strangest seventh inning show I've ever seen," Adam whispered to Helen as they watched Thoreau play tic-tac-toe against his heirloom chicken.

"Stay weird, Portland."

Thoreau won the game and hugged the fowl.

It was so nice, so normal, conferring with her, chatting. It was sort of like they were spending the day together, even though the circumstances were strange. Then again, oddness seemed to draw them together. He liked the crisp air and the breeze. Someone handed him a soy dog, and it tasted delicious. He liked the way Helen talked so comfortably to all of the kids and to the anxious parents. They almost seemed like a normal couple on a date. A date where they were judging poultry.

Finally, the chair of the hospital board came to them with ribbons and envelopes. It looked like there were plenty of prizes. "Oh, good, something for everyone," Adam said, relieved.

"I thought you'd love the opportunity to judge some livestock, Farm Boy."

She nudged him, and her eyes glittered with laughter. He felt his heart swell.

They had a word with each kid to talk about how great they all were, and it took a while to talk about that. A cheer went up for the exceptional chickens *and* children. By the time Adam jogged back to join his team, the weather had gotten colder and his muscles were stiff. He felt great.

The game resumed. Sort of. Helen went back to the outfield. Golfer came up to bat determined to outshine everyone, it seemed. Maybe he was the Exceptional Chicken. After testing a couple of bats, he was now attempting to juggle them, swinging them high into the air so that he could have enough time to catch them. "What's he doing now?" Serge exclaimed next to him. "Does he think this is some kind of carnival?"

"Can you blame him for thinking that?" asked Soccer Guy.

As Golfer moved farther and farther away from home plate, the Docs started to shift from their positions nervously.

But then, of course, Doctor Sandy-Hair yelled something at Helen, which caused her to jog up to the pitcher's mound. And the asshole Golfer started to lose control. Instead of throwing it straight up, the heavy wood went right across the field, and even before Adam could start to run for her, before he could shout a warning, the bat came down on Helen's head.

Chapter Thirteen

It's a good thing there are a lot of doctors here, was a thought that Helen had never expected to have, ever. She couldn't keep her eyes open. Or were they closed already? There was too much light intruding, too much shouting. Her head tingled. It wasn't even pain, it was just too much feeling. Someone warm and smelling faintly of Icy Hot was touching her shoulders. *Adam*, she thought. She was glad it was him. But he wouldn't know what to do with her, how to help.

She had to tell him what to do. "I think I have a concussion," she mumbled.

Or maybe she didn't.

–

Adam was supposed to get on a plane in the morning to fly out to New York for a series of road games, then go home briefly for the holidays, but with Helen in hospital, he didn't want to leave the city.

He paced his apartment. Of course, he wasn't haunting her bedside. They weren't anything to each other, and she was hardly alone. Practically the whole hospital had been watching as that bat came at her. She had her friends and colleagues and any number of people wanting to soothe and cure her. He probably shouldn't have bolted ahead of the doctors who were trying to help. He'd only gotten to touch her for a few minutes before they took her away, just long enough for her to murmur something to him. He thought she said concussion. But maybe it was just a word he expected to hear from her. He couldn't even say anything back because his throat was clogged with worry.

Petra had been the one to turn him away, though. And Serge had made him go home.

So he went home.

Despite Petra's distraction, she'd promised to text him. Helen's friend had been the only one who could reason with him and reassure him. She knew exactly what to do, like almost everyone else there – everyone except him. And the golfer, who had retreated in ignominy.

If Adam ever saw the golfer again, he was going to break every single stick in his bag. Then he would do the same to Dr. Sandy Hair. The man probably had lots of expensive golf clubs to break because he was just that kind of asshole. There had been no need for Dr. Sandy Hair to call Helen up and put her in the line of fire.

Adam clenched his fists. He checked his phone again. Nothing from Petra since she'd texted to say the diagnosis had been concussion. *Just like Helen said*, he thought.

He wondered how much pain she felt. The last time he'd had a concussion, even lying in bed staring at the ceiling made him dizzy. His own head throbbed with tension just imagining her confused and hurt.

He thought about what Helen had said about her father, about how close she had been to him, how helpless she must feel, and the powerlessness crawled through his hands until he noticed that he was gripping the damp sheets. *This is what it feels like to be on the other side*, he thought. Watching and waiting, living in suspense over the pains suffered by someone else.

He wondered how she managed to do it – not just with her father, but with all of her patients. What would it be like to be responsible for so many people? What would it be like to watch people deteriorate? What would it be like to live with that frustration all the time, especially for someone as vital as Helen? What did she do with all that energy?

He gave up on sleep. He smoothed the sheets as best he could, rechecked his luggage, and then he logged on to his computer.

He thought he'd put the worst parts of his life behind him: the drinking, the near bankruptcy. But tonight, he felt bad – too bad to sleep, too bad to stay up. And he hadn't even been hit.

–

So this is what it felt like to receive karmic justice, Helen thought, her eyes closed. For future reference: karmic justice felt a lot like a concussion.

She felt confused and slow, and she had a headache threading like a loud, persistent argument through her skull. Sometimes, she couldn't remember how she'd gotten in the hospital – or that it was a hospital. It was better to stay asleep, to lie in this strange bed while other people took care of her, to not be able to sustain a thought for very long before sinking into dreams. Her colleagues came in to wake her at regular intervals. Petra was there and Joanie and Sarah. She woke up groggily at one point and wondered where her family was, then realized they were in Canada. She remembered her dad was sick. It was better when she forgot.

Petra had dealt with the paperwork the night before and called Helen's brother. She texted updates to a list of people and pushed visitors out. It was easy for her friends who were hospital personnel to overstay their welcomes. They were used to remaining in rooms exactly as long as they thought they should. But Petra was firm.

But early the next day, when the nurse helped Helen sign out, Helen thought that she remembered that Adam had also been with her – held her – so briefly she wasn't sure it was real. She felt something, though, almost as if he'd left the smallest dent in her just by putting his warm hands on her. And now he wasn't there, and those imprints he'd left on her ached.

When Sarah arrived to drive her home, she brought Helen a change of clothing and a huge green drink.

"What is it?" Helen asked, suspiciously.

"It's my latest. I call it *Epic Kale*."

Helen took a sniff. "You realize that I almost died recently."

"Yeah. I heard you were wearing your tiger-striped leggings. You know my policy: Never wear anything you could potentially be caught dead in."

Sarah checked her seatbelt.

Helen said, "Just for that, I'm updating my will to reflect that I wish to be buried in those leggings. And I want an open casket funeral."

The sweater and yoga pants that Sarah had brought Helen were comfortable and perfect, although she was not going to tell her friend that. She took a cautious sip of the juice and peeked at herself in the mirror. Her face wasn't terrible, she thought, touching it gingerly. She would have a scar on her forehead, and there would be yellow and purple bruising for days. She liked it. It was just a little unexpected, a little unfamiliar, much like this kale juice.

"I don't think *Epic Kale* is the right name for this," said Helen. "Maybe, *It Kaled Have Been Worse*. Or *Kale Me Now*."

"That doesn't even make sense," Sarah muttered, fiddling with the GPS.

"GPS? Are you serious? It's my house. You've been there millions of times."

Sarah turned the ignition. "Well, *someone's* obviously feeling better."

They rode in silence for a while. Then Sarah said, very casually, "I heard that Adam Magnus pushed people out of the way to reach you."

"I wouldn't know if he did," said Helen.

She felt a warm gush of pleasure to have it confirmed, though. Another one of those, and she'd be leaking all over Sarah's pristine car. She blinked and shielded her eyes, telling herself that the sun was making her head hurt.

Sarah had snapped into work talk now. She said something about rearranging office schedules with Joanie and something about hospital shifts. All Helen heard was that she was covered and that she didn't have to do anything for a few days.

Sarah had planted the Adam seed on purpose, damn her.

Adam had run to her. Despite all she'd done, despite all the stupid things she'd told him, he had rushed to her side. She hoped that he'd punched that obnoxious showboating golfer. And Dr. Al McGinnis. She hoped that he'd shoved Al McGinnis down like a screaming derby-girl banshee.

Not that she advocated violence.

She felt irrational laughter floating to the top of her stomach. Her head was fuzzing again, and she hoped Sarah was keeping track of the meds, because Helen felt close to becoming a giggling, crying mess. It wasn't the pain, so much, as it was her vulnerability. Disconcertingly, she wished that Adam were at her apartment, waiting for her. He would be so warm and comforting. A hard fist of desire settled among all the other jangling physical feelings, and she concentrated on trying not to whimper.

Her head jerked up.

They rounded the corner onto her street. The GPS was talking to Sarah as if she were a very young child, albeit one with a sophisticated understanding of measurements.

But Adam hadn't come to see her today. He couldn't last night, of course. He wasn't even her boyfriend. He didn't even know her number. She didn't know his. It was probably better for her pride if she didn't have it because she'd probably call him and blubber and pass out midsentence. But she didn't care about her pride at that moment.

The car came to a stop, and Helen gritted her teeth.

"Just two minutes and we'll be inside, and you'll be able to take your drugs," Sarah said.

Damn Sarah for being too perceptive.

Helen stumbled out of the car and held on to the roof.

Petra was waiting inside. "I had Ian send food from the restaurant," she said.

"Bed, just bed," Helen muttered.

She didn't even want to move her lips.

Her friends helped her up the stairs. Petra doled out the meds, and Sarah slung her into pajamas. They drew the blinds.

She wanted to tell them that she didn't need a babysitter, she was a brain doctor, and she knew exactly what was wrong with her and what she had to do. But what she had to do included having them stay with her. They wouldn't have listened anyway. And she didn't really want them to go.

Chapter Fourteen

By the next afternoon, Helen was starting to feel a little stir crazy. She was tired of wearing flannel pajamas and clicking listlessly through the television channels – not that she was supposed to watch too much TV. She was well enough to be on her own now, but she still needed bed rest. What a crock. Forget about cures for progressive brain degeneration, forget about concussion and hockey: When she was better, she was going to expose the stupidity of rest and recovery. Because all that idle time led to brooding, and brooding led to regrets, and regrets were really terrible and useless.

The problem was, she knew all the rules for dealing with concussion, and that made her want to flout every single one of them. She wanted to stand on her head or do cartwheels across her living room. She wanted to stay up all night playing video games and bike to the office. She wanted to blare Beyoncé and dance around her kitchen shout-screaming the lyrics. She wanted to check the statistical analysis on the cervical spine-injury study that she and her colleagues in the neurology department had started, despite the fact that it wasn't her job – she wanted to get obnoxious about the numbers and yell at the study statistician even though she knew she wouldn't win. She even wanted to do her practice paperwork so that she could rail at the insurance company, for God's sake.

But her own body kept betraying her. She would sit down and try to read or think, and her concentration would wander. She would get indignant only to have the outrage die away when she got too tired. The only thing she managed to do was sleep and watch TCM. Every time she woke up, she was in the middle of a different black and white movie.

It would have been easy to start watching hockey again, she thought, sitting in her bathtub. But Adam hadn't contacted her, even though she suspected that he should be able to find a way if he wanted to – she could probably get his number if she tried. But she didn't. And she didn't watch any of the games, although she did check the Wolves' schedule and learn that they were on an extended road trip. That made her feel a little better.

She did not have a crush on him. Except, she probably did.

She also did not sit in the cool water of her bathtub and think of how his lips felt on her shoulder and neck or imagine her fingers passing over the soft bristles of his hair and wonder how they would feel wet. Except, of course, she did.

She thought of how his big hands cupped her ass and drew her to him, how gentle his fingers had been, the feeling of his breath on her chest. Her middle and index finger were trilling at her clit now. She had to stop thinking about him, she told herself, midstroke. Desperately, she replaced Adam with someone – anyone. Zachary Quinto. Christian Bale. The guy who invented the Dyson vacuum cleaner. The water splashed as she worked herself tensely. But although the painful knot of arousal was there, her mind kept going back to Adam, to his pale eyes and his rueful smile. She pictured his lips curving up at her breast, and she threw her head back and came with a series of splashes. Her panting seemed to echo in the bathroom.

Almost immediately – while her muscles were still calming themselves – she picked up a bar of pale green soap and began washing the hand she'd been using. She cleaned under her fingernails and sniffed to make sure that her scent was gone. It wasn't. Her fingers smelled like cucumber and self-pleasure.

Sex salad. Just what she'd ordered.

She stepped out and heard someone downstairs. She toweled herself off and threw on a clean sweatshirt and another not-so-immaculate pair of yoga pants. It was Joanie.

"This came for you at the office," Joanie said, pushing a box toward her. "It's Harry & David! Open it up!"

Inside was a box of salty caramel popcorn.

"Wow, whoever sent it really knows you," Joanie said.

Joanie looked at it longingly. She was on some sort of complicated diet that involved juicing. She and Sarah had a lot to talk about during off hours.

"Wasn't there a card?" Helen asked.

She checked the box. *Adam Magnus*, the gift slip said. No message.

Helen's face flamed. She stared at the box, feeling a little as if masturbating to his image had conjured up a big package of sweet and crunchy. Had she psychically contacted him across thousands of miles? If so, should she expect similar packages from Dyson guy?

She took a deep breath, and her inner scientist reasserted herself. The more important question was when had she mentioned her love of popcorn? Or was it simply a coincidence?

The next morning, Petra ferried over a delivery of artisanal Pop-Tarts that had come to the office from Adam. She also mentioned, casually, that she had texted Adam to assure him that Helen was doing well enough to be on her own now.

So yes, Helen admitted to herself, he knew certain things about her. He'd recalled bits that she'd dropped in casual conversation. *No damage to that memory*. Petra or Sarah might have gotten her these kinds of snacks, if they thought it would make her happy, or if they thought she was as unhappy as she was. Although, they were more likely to simply bring her the real thing, in grocery bags, from an ordinary store. Adam's presents had a *moreness* to them. The extra salty sweet layer of the popcorn, the rough-hewn edges of the homemade Pop-Tarts – they were about her, but they were also about him. If she cared to read more into them, that was. It was funny to think of Adam, hunched over his iPhone, ordering treats for her. The gestures were, well, almost romantic. Which suited her idea of Adam Magnus, she supposed. He could produce small acts of delicacy with that large body of his.

Definitely reading too much into it, she thought with a shiver.

Thank God she was going back to work tomorrow, because she would likely spend the day diddling herself and muttering his name if she didn't have something to occupy her hands and mind soon. She supposed that she should write some sort of thank-you note: *I appreciate the gifts. So thoughtful for you to have remembered! My many fond memories of you have caused me to rub one out – several, actually. Looking forward to more lively debates! Helen.*

Oh yes, she had just the stationary for that.

The caramel corn was really delicious.

She racked her addled brain for a gift. What did she know about him? He had been a farm boy; he sang in the choir. He was pretty good at softball. Something about seraphim and cherubim.

A Google search revealed some music by Handel. She listened to the choruses, and tried to imagine a young, skinny Adam Magnus, standing in the midst of a choir, singing his heart out. She could almost picture white blond hair, ears that stuck out a little too much, and an eager mouth opening wide. The image made her breast-bone ache. With a few clicks, she had downloaded him a Christmas present. If only she could figure out his e-mail address so she could send the music.

Because yes, it was almost Christmas. Her ticket home was booked, and she felt guilty that she had already taken so much time from work. But home could not be avoided either. Her mother would have her head on a platter, decorated with cranberries, Helen supposed, to suit the season.

Home. Well. Vancouver was where she would slink off to now. Stephen and Gordon had probably decked out their home in tasteful white lights. But the holidays had never been a huge deal in their family. Her father was usually on call, and her mother turned her nose up at red and green decorations, loathed cooking large, bland potato-based meals, and didn't believe in giving presents to children without ample reason. So basically, May Yin and Harry Frobisher disliked everything about it. Still, Helen had enjoyed it because she was at home, sitting in the den, watching old movies with Stephen. They would both drowse under several layers of afghans, because her parents were of the "If you're cold, put on another sweater," mentality. And she and Stephen were always cold.

But now, that old house was cleared of furniture. The piano that her father wanted her to have, sold. There was no reason to drive down to the Okanagan Valley anymore. Likely, they would just go out to dinner on Christmas, and there would be no snuggling. Stephen and Gordon kept their place at a reasonable temperature, partly because, Helen suspected, they liked to go around in tight T-shirts and stare at each other's pecs.

But really, she was happy for them.

There would also be her father. Christmas was probably garish and loud in the facility. Her mother might have to listen to carols, and her father would be confused. Were they allowed to check him out for the day? She wondered if they would be able to stay in the facility. She wondered how much he knew about what was going on at this point.

She wished she could stay in Portland.

Adam Magnus, she supposed, was going back to Minnesota. He hadn't told her much about his family, but she could imagine snow-covered fields and a big farmhouse.

She had a sudden impulse to talk to him. Petra had mentioned casually (maybe a little too casually) that she had Adam's number. Helen needed to thank him, and she wanted to know where to send these mp3s, anyway.

She texted Petra and held her breath.

–

"I could spread the rumor that Yevgeny paid the golfer to finish her off, and that when the golfer didn't do it, you tried to clean up and you pushed a bunch of people aside in order to hug her to death," Serge said.

Silence.

Serge had been talking, talking, talking over the drone of the plane for hours, it seemed, and Adam had not responded. The cabin lights were dim, and most of his teammates were asleep. A few watched movies on their phones. They would land in about twenty minutes. The Wolves had lost two games, and now they were off to Minnesota. Adam's family would be in the arena – his nephews, his brother and sister, even his mother and father. He would try to go out with them afterward, but they had a long drive and were early risers and he was sure to be tired. Judging by the exhausted silence that hung around them after his games, he wondered why they insisted on seeing him. There was nothing quite like the cranky, dutiful love of one's family, was there?

It wasn't that he disliked them. They weren't unpleasant. But they treated him gingerly. He wondered exactly what he had done to merit this treatment.

Plus, he would be back so soon for Christmas. He had already found great presents for his nephews.

Personal toy shopper, he thought. That could be a career.

He told himself to make a note of it in his smart phone, but he didn't move.

Adam wasn't sure why Janel was so annoyed with him. Yevgeny wasn't distressed with Adam – or at least Adam hadn't received any sneering e-mails or phone calls from his big billionaire boss. Plus, a picture of Helen Frobisher dressed in those ugly leggings shaking the hands of the hospital chair and her anti-Yevgeny developer husband was making the rounds, too.

Of course, all of the gossip and innuendo was playing out in the admittedly narrow circle of Portland municipal politics. Frankly, Adam was surprised that Yevgeny even bothered trying to win in that arena.

Serge was still nattering. "I suppose Dr. Helen is going to argue that we ban charity softball, too. Maybe golf. Definitely golf. Is it even a sport? Of course, now that she has a brain injury, you could tell Yevgeny to start a campaign questioning her judgment."

"I'm sure that's already underway."

"Well then, Janel's doing a great job diverting the argument."

They landed smoothly, and they made it off the plane fairly quickly.

Adam breathed in the air of his home state.

Outside the large windows of the airport, snow glittered on the ground like diamonds. He used to like the Minneapolis-St. Paul airport. It was large and airy, like a giant art gallery. It was the kind of place that made one feel simultaneously larger and so much smaller. There was life everywhere, but somehow muted, as if the midwestern attitude had just taken everything to a civilized notch.

But still, he felt that familiar guilt settle over him. The air was layered with the sense of his failure, pushing down on his chest, making it hard to breathe.

The players were hushed as they came out into the chilly air and then shuttled to their hotel. Adam had just put his luggage down in his room when his phone beeped. He read,

> IT'S HELEN. WHAT IS YOUR E-MAIL
> ADDRESS?

He had to read the simple message several times because he couldn't quite believe it was Helen – *his* Helen. On screen, her name looked so simple compared to the complicated feelings she summoned up. He told himself to stay cool.

> IT'S MADAMIMMAGNUS@GMAIL.COM. WHY NOT JUST TEXT?

Her reply came with an eyeroll emoji.

> I DON'T WANT TO GET MY PHONE STICKY WITH DELICIOUS CARAMEL CORN.

He snorted.

> IS THAT SUPPOSED TO BE A THANK-YOU?

He heard the ping of a message to his e-mail account just as her answer came.

> INCOMING E-MAIL IS THE THANK-YOU. GOTTA GO.

He opened his e-mail. There was a file attached. He downloaded the file and clicked. The music of strings started up, and then the voices, the beautiful voices, flooded the room.

He sat down on the hotel room bed, and he listened.

Chapter Fifteen

"I am trying not to feel weird about the fact that I essentially made a mixtape for you filled with sacred music," Helen said into the phone.

It was late at night. She was in her bedroom, sorting through a pile of laundry. She had put the phone on speaker. Tomorrow, she planned to go back into work.

Adam had called her later that afternoon. Now she had dialed him up. It was very late in Minneapolis, and he sounded tired.

Their conversations had started out odd, stilted. She felt as if she were always on the verge of blurting something overly confessional to him within the first few minutes. There was so much more that she wanted to tell him, despite the fact that their acquaintance didn't warrant this level of naked feeling. Or did it? She had kissed him and had sex with him, after all – it didn't get more naked than that. But no, that wasn't it. She had told him a secret about her relationship with her father that she hadn't known was a secret. He'd tried to soothe her when she was injured.

"It wouldn't be the first time a woman did that for me," Adam said. "Although I don't know if I would classify a tape filled with Rebecca St. James songs as *sacred*, even if it was Christian rock."

"I have never heard of Rebecca St. James. Who gave you that?"

"A high-school girlfriend."

Helen paused for a bit. She picked up a pair of boy shorts and folded it into tiny, tiny squares. "Did she put out?" she said, because it was fairly close to the question that she wanted to ask.

Adam laughed. "No," he said. "And I was okay with that. Or rather, I wasn't, like, delighted about it, because my hormones were hopped up and frankly terrifying. I was barely fifteen, and I was a mess. But we got over each other fairly quickly. I remember the tape – CD actually – though, because she'd made a collage of hockey sticks and Jesus and hearts—"

"Oh my God."

"Exactly."

They laughed uncomfortably.

Helen sat on the bed cross-legged.

"How does it feel to beat people up?" Helen asked.

The line was quiet for a while.

"I'm not trying to antagonize," Helen said. "It's just… I watched the game tonight. And I can't help but think about it every time you start circling someone with your skates. He circles back, and I look at the screen and my stomach drops. I can't read your expression. Are you tense? Are you scared? What do you think is going to happen? It's hard for me to watch, sometimes." She laughed. "Every time. But then I can't look away."

Another pause.

"What are you doing now?" Helen asked softly.

"I'm sitting on the hotel bed. I'm icing my knee, again. And I'm trying to think of what I'm thinking when that happens."

"When *that* happens," Helen said, lightly. "You sound as if you're not in control of it, like it just is this whirlpool that draws you in."

"It's like that, in a way. I mean, I'm very aware of the things going on around me, the sound of my skates on the ice. I'm looking at where his stick is, and where the other players on his team are. I'm staring at him to see how much this means to him, too. Like, are you going to pull that move again? Am I really going to have to go in there? Does everyone expect it right now? And sometimes, I feel how tired I am. And if I've been playing awhile, I'm wondering how much of what I'm doing is a warning. I'm gauging if what I'm doing is enough. If by simply stopping to look at him, it's enough."

"It sounds like a complicated calculation."

"It is. A calculation and a ritual, in a way. But it only takes a few seconds. And the whole time it's happening, my adrenaline is pumping in anticipation of a blow."

Helen swallowed. "Sometimes I feel like I'd really like to beat someone up," she said. "What's worse, it's usually... well, I was in the hospital elevator after biking to work last week and I saw a man in a bowtie, and I wondered, what would it be like to kick his head in? I felt like I could really do some damage. And then I could assess the damage, speaking as a neurologist, of course."

Adam laughed a little. "I didn't know women had these feelings that often."

"What's that supposed to mean?"

"Like, random physical aggression. The desire to test out your impact, maybe."

"Well, I don't like speaking for all women, so I'll just say all people do, and it depends on their personality."

"Well, I like speaking for all men," said Adam. "I like to think I'm in charge or that I could run things better."

He sounded relaxed now.

"No, violence doesn't have to be a series of sudden blows, I think. I mean, when I danced, I hurt all the time. I developed a condition called female athlete triad, which was amenorrhea, disordered eating, and osteoporosis. Um… I never was anorexic. I definitely ate." She winced, knowing she sounded defensive. "But yeah, my bones became thin, and I tore my ACL, and I had to quit because I was—"

She couldn't finish.

"Anyway," she said.

"Helen."

"Dancing looked beautiful. But for me, anyway – not for everyone, but for me – it was also painful, and it was good for me to get out of it. I know it's not anything compared to the abuse that other people, other women, suffer the world over. But it was a slow violence for me, and it came from expectations that other people had and that I had of myself."

They were both quiet for a minute.

"Thank you," he said, and his voice was so gentle that she felt calm again.

They talked a lot over the next few nights, between her shifts, after games, in their separate, very separate, beds. She didn't know what it was. She didn't know what they were doing. It wasn't friendship. It was too sex-tinged to be that simple or complicated. On more than one night, she ended up with her hand down her pants while on the phone with him. Afterward, they laughed self-consciously, still a little awkward, still unsure.

He wasn't the person she thought he was, she thought as she arrived in the hospital parking lot a few days later. It was now her last day before she took off for Vancouver. He was set to fly back to Minnesota. She wondered, although not aloud, if the phone conversations would continue.

Of course, now she couldn't exactly remember what kind of person she had thought he was, because over the course of a handful of conversations in which she bossed him about his minor injuries, and he made fun of her eating habits, she could not imagine not seeing the angles of him. It had been there from the start: the easy way he laughed at himself, his refusal to back down from her – but she had refused that, and now she wondered how she could have been so blind. He wasn't noisy, but that didn't mean he didn't have mental strength. He didn't assert himself in an obvious way, and she had been content to go with her own story of him. But he had been there, all along, his bass notes playing the counterpoint to her wheedling melodies, until finally she acknowledged him, until finally they approached the middle.

–

Adam was home, at the farm, and he had been up early. Cows didn't stop for Christmas, and besides, he had volunteered his services. His nephews had woken in anticipation of presents. They were whooping around the living room, shooting each other with rocket blasters and pelting action figures at each other. The sound of sturdy feet running back and forth and soft thuds as volleys of tiny, crushable, easy-to-lose plastic weapons carpeted the family room. Half-transformed robots stuck up like buoys from between the couch cushions. Despite his tiredness, he really did feel like the best uncle ever.

Outside, it was still dark, but the house was ablaze with light. His dad was sitting in an armchair in the den, watching TV at a high volume. He hadn't run the farm in years, now. "But let's not talk about politics on a day like this," said the news anchor. He began to talk about politics.

They sat silently for a while, Adam and his dad, drinking weak coffee from chipped mugs. It was probably impossible to converse over the sound of the program anyway. And they had never been much for chatting.

His dad looked a little better, actually. He had always been tall, but he had put on a little weight so that he didn't have the shriveled pocket mouth that the older members of the Magnus family sometimes got. Adam hadn't expected retirement to agree with the old man.

Helen's father had barely gotten to enjoy his retirement. He wondered what Helen was doing with her father and her family. He wondered how she was coping.

He'd looked up female athlete triad when they'd gotten off the phone.

As he tuned out the voices coming at him from the TV, the shouts of his nephews, the crash of pans from the kitchen, he started to feel angry on her behalf.

So much about her was thrown into relief with every conversation they'd had: her regrets, her fierce desire to protect people from illness, her fear about her father. She had not known what was going on; she had been helpless. She had been alone and young in a strange city. She thought she was cosseted in the glass world of ballet, and that all she had to do was work hard and be talented, but her body had eaten away at itself, and the protection of her art had been no protection at all. She had lost what she wanted to do and forced herself to start over. She was strong, but frankly, he was angry that she had to be strong.

It was funny how she could be completely blunt with him and yet so guarded. Maybe it was because he already knew her on some level. She hadn't sounded like herself last night. Seeing her father, having endless rounds of conversation with her mother and brother were wearing her down. She didn't have her usual snap. He had begun to be able to interpret the moods of her pauses and avoided answers. Skimming his fingers over the bumps of their conversation, he read the sadness underneath.

Maybe he should call her.

His father interrupted his thoughts. "Your team isn't very good," his father said. "But, like I always told you, it's better to work hard than to be talented. Or smart."

His father had said nothing of the sort. He'd barely spoken ten words to him in the last two decades. This already seemed like the longest conversation they'd ever had. Adam had no idea why it was happening. Then again, he'd never really hung out with his dad. There had always been too much to do in the mornings. Maybe the long days ground his father down into a little nub.

Adam sipped his coffee.

"I'll be retiring pretty soon," he said, testing out his dad's reaction.

His father grunted.

"Although, the owner, Yevgeny Molotov, said he'd consider me for some work in his organization."

"Billionaires." His father spat the word out. "Everyone throws that number around now. That kind of wealth is mirrors and shadows. You can't sink your future into that."

Well, that wasn't too encouraging.

"I could give you a share of the farm," his father said conversationally.

Adam didn't know if the man even knew what he was saying. The farm was his sister's. She'd been working it for years. Her whole life was in it. Somehow, *No, thanks*, didn't quite seem adequate. Although it would have been as casual as his father's dismissal of his sister's work. "It belongs to Jennifer and her family, Dad. I'm also applying to go back to school," he added.

His father grunted again.

Luckily, his nephew scrambled on top of the couch. "This popped out, Uncle Adam."

The kid held up a figurine and a leg. He'd only received it this morning. Adam took the leg and the plastic torso and peered at it. Were his eyes going, along with everything else? He put the pieces together and squeezed gently, afraid of breaking the toy. Nothing happened.

"Here, let me," his father said gruffly. Dad's hands were surprisingly steady. "There's one thing I can still do around here."

But he looked pleased, and Lyle was pressed up against his grandfather's leg now, explaining about the superhero's powers. The kid talked a mile a minute, and here, Dad's grunts seemed entirely appropriate. Those two really liked each other, Adam realized, looking at the two heads now close together. Maybe his dad had found his place, after all. It had taken him a few wrong turns, but life had given his father many chances.

Unexpectedly shaken by the thought, Adam got up. He was going to make his way to the kitchen when his phone rang. It was Helen. It was really early in Vancouver, Canada. "Merry holiday," she said. "Greetings of the goddess upon you."

"Are you waving pine branches around and wearing a bedsheet?"

"Wouldn't you like to know what I'm wearing?" she said, her voice thick and dark.

Oh. It was *that* kind of conversation. He smiled.

"We could Facetime," Adam said.

"It's too dark here, and I'm not turning on any lights. My mother has a sixth sense about this kind of thing."

His nephew, Jake, whirred past him. He needed to find a more private spot, but with everyone gathered at the house, that seemed unlikely. His brother-in-law was in the basement watching that hockey movie with Kurt Russell in very loud jackets; his mother was in the kitchen basting obsessively; and his sister was yelling at the kids, wrangling the dog, and holding scraps of wrapping paper. He had two choices: He could go outside and maybe into one of the outbuildings and possibly freeze to death, or he could go to his room, which, thankfully had changed since he'd last inhabited it. At least he wouldn't feel like a teenager masturbating furtively in his room.

Now he was an adult about to masturbate furtively in his room – that is, if he was lucky.

"Where are you now? Isn't it awfully early?"

"I'm in the guest room. Everyone's still asleep. No kids to wake us up. Although, I think they're thinking of adopting. They're going to have to loosen up, though. I don't think that white suede couch is going to stand up very well to grubby hands."

"How is your dad?" he asked.

"Sleep disturbances, probably due to his new surroundings, accompanied by the expected deterioration of his motor skills," she said distantly.

"And your mom?"

"Fine. Worried. But relieved."

A pause.

"So, what are *you* wearing?" she asked.

"A red bow and a sprig of mistletoe between my teeth?"

"Nice. Where's the bow?"

"It's strategically placed across my left shin, of course."

Helen laughed, a light tapping sound. He tried to hold the phone tighter to his ear as he checked the lock of his door.

"What are you really wearing?" she asked.

"Jeans, a plaid shirt."

"Farm boy fashion. Are you buttoned all the way to the top, or can I see a little of that chest fuzz peeking through?"

He settled on the bed and looked down. "Some hair. Are you sure you want to do this?"

"It feels a little weird," she admitted. "But I need this."

An answering yearning twisted inside him.

"Okay, then let's just go slow. We'll narrate as much as we can. We have all morning, if we need to."

He heard a little rustling.

"I was taking off some of my clothing," she said. "I'm getting under the sheets." She laughed shakily. "God, I feel like I'm broadcasting. It seems so loud."

"No one else can hear us just talking. It's not like we're on walkie-talkies, where we have to end everything with, *Roger this, roger that, roger yourself.*"

She sighed, and his already stirring cock stiffened. "I know," she said. "But I'm going to hide my head under the covers anyway."

"Are you naked?" he asked, gritting his teeth. It had been far too long since he'd seen her naked.

"I'm wearing a tank top."

"Is it tight?"

"Oh, so tight."

"What is it about hearing you say that, even when I know you're joking, that makes me feel like I'm going to burst?"

"Burst how?"

"Like I have no more blood or muscle left in the rest of my body, like I have no more thoughts, like the planet begins and ends with my balls and their gravitational pull. And your voice is the warm currents of air, wafting over them."

It was her turn to suck in a breath. "I don't know whether that's astoundingly vulgar or poetic or just plain full bullshit."

"Probably all of that. I feel full of everything right now, but still unsatisfied."

She laughed, another puff of breath that he could almost feel over his cheek. His grip on the phone tightened, and he moved his fingers over it convulsively.

"Are you unzipped?"

He was, but he wasn't touching anything. It would be too much.

He tried to divert.

"What are you doing?" he asked.

"Flapping the covers," she said. "I'm trying to get a little air under here. I don't want anyone to hear, but it's too hot and it's dark and I'm damp and I feel like I'm a teenager doing something illicit."

"Lick your fingers," he said.

He could almost imagine the parting of her lips, the press of her nail on her pliable tongue, the click of wetness on the pad of her fingers, one, after another, after another.

"Draw your fingers down your neck, trail them down to your nipple," he said.

"I'm circling it," she whispered.

"I'm taking it in my mouth and sucking and nipping. And now I'm moving down your stomach. I'm licking your belly button."

He had to unzip and touch himself now. "Imagine my hands sliding down your thighs. I love your thighs, that long deep groove of muscle along the side. If I smooth my thumbs along them just right, I can make your legs fall open."

"They're open," she said.

"Can you see my head between your legs?" he said.

"Your blond hair. I always think it's going to be spiky, but it's so smooth, and it springs up against my hand as I smooth it back, a thousand tiny touches."

She sounded soft and helpless. He was trying to hold back, but his hand pumped his cock faster and faster.

"Imagine your hand on my head, my tongue and lips kissing your sweet clit."

"It's not really sweet, is it?"

"Sweet as honey crisp apples, sweet like maple syrup and birthday cake with rainbow sprinkles."

She snorted, which was maybe not the reaction one wanted to elicit during phone sex.

"Scratch that. You taste more sort of... elemental," he added. "Bring your fingers up so you can find out for yourself," he said.

Her breathing was audible now and a little unsteady. "I'm licking my own fingers," she said, a laugh in her voice. "I didn't think I'd like it. But I'm pretending it's your tongue on me. You're looking at me, pausing to describe what I taste like without giving me a hard time. Then winking at me."

"I sound like a cocky devil. Are you sure it's me you're picturing?"

"Yes," she said on another breath. "Yes, it's definitely you. Your pale eyes, your big hands curving over my thighs, your mouth, your lips, your tongue in me."

Oh, he felt that one. So did she.

"I want you to fuck me," she hissed, almost adamant. "I wish I could feel you inside me."

"Fuck yourself. Use your fingers."

"I am."

They were both moving faster now; they were getting louder and trying to restrain themselves. A few incoherent sounds came from him, and he almost dropped the phone.

And then, to his relief, he could hear her come right then, her gasping, the sheets flapping against the receiver as she bucked. And he turned himself over and buried his face into a pillow, grabbing it with his teeth to muffle the sound, and he came into the clean cotton duvet.

Apparently, he'd have a late night of secret laundry.

He couldn't wait to get back to Portland.

Chapter Sixteen

"You'd think a neurologist would be better at avoiding a concussion," her patient Mr. Lake sniffed, by way of welcome.

She had spent enough time in Vancouver. A few more days of wandering restlessly around downtown, shopping with Gordon and her mother, brooding with her father, and talking as quietly with Adam as she could manage. And now she was back and healed, and it all seemed a lifetime ago that she had missed that last appointment with Mr. Lake. He seemed unlikely to let her forget it.

"Well, I wasn't trying to get cracked in the head with a bat," Helen said. "How have you been this month?"

"You knew the dangers," Mr. Lake insisted, opening his eyes wide. "Softball can be a very hazardous sport, notwithstanding the name."

She was never going to live this down, she thought, jabbing grimly at her iPhone. "Let's take a look at your headache diary," she said.

At the end of the exam, she walked Mr. Lake out and found Adam standing outside her door. Her heart gave a painful throb as they just stood and stared at each other.

"Look, it's your nemesis, the big goon. Here to finish the job?" Mr. Lake asked.

Sarah took the wrong moment to stride out of her office. She took a wide-legged stance in the hallway, her eyes darting between Mr. Lake and Adam. Clearly, she sensed something was up. She came, maybe, up to Adam's elbow.

"Everything okay here?" she asked Helen.

Adam looked over Sarah at her, and Helen's chest squeezed painfully. "Everything's fine," she croaked.

After talking to Adam for so long on the phone, it was almost difficult to be faced with his immense physical presence. She had forgotten about the golden haze of stubble that made his jaw seem to glow, his arms, his lips, the phosphorescence of his pale eyes as they took her in. He was magnificent. She should probably save him from Mr. Lake, though.

"Helen can take care of herself," Adam was saying, half amused, half fearful.

"Doc Frobisher is *Canadian*," Mr. Lake said.

"Are you really trying to convince a hockey player that Canadians are a peaceful, unaggressive people?"

Her patient still looked tense. Helen said, "Mr. Lake, despite the rumors you may have heard, Adam's a… a friend. We're not really enemies, even though we sometimes debate each other. It's, ah, healthy disagreement."

Adam flitted his eyes over at her and quirked his mouth. She was turning red. She hardly ever blushed, and so she had never realized how uncomfortable it was. Even her shoulder blades pricked with heat. She was going to set the office on fire, and the water cooler was at least three feet away from her.

"I got in early. Your office is near my apartment. I thought I'd just drop in and see... you," Adam said.

"Oh. I see how it is," Mr. Lake said.

Mr. Lake didn't move.

At least Sarah was enjoying the show, though. She was trying to stifle a giggle even as Helen grew more uncomfortable. Sarah flicked her gaze at Adam and gave him an *I see you and I'm going to ask you a million questions later* smile before shutting herself in her office. They all heard her chortle from behind the door.

Mr. Lake on the other hand showed no signs of leaving. He had been Helen's last patient of the day. "Erm, so you've already got your next appointment scheduled?" Helen asked him.

"I do, Doctor."

"And... you have any questions for me?"

"No. I've got the drill down."

Helen nodded. "Great." She thought for a minute. "Well, have a good night, Mr. Lake." She turned to Adam. "Mr. Magnus, would you like to come into my office?"

"Your entire crew is made up of elderly patients and tiny women," he said in her ear.

"Pretty much."

She opened the door for him and let him enter first.

They stood still for a minute.

"Do you think they're still listening?" Adam whispered.

He took a step toward her and brought up his hand to the side of her breast, his fingers hesitating just short of her coat.

"That's a bold move," she murmured, stepping into his grasp.

She put her hand on his chest. "It's nothing compared to what I want to do with you," he said, stroking her softly. "I wasn't quite sure what my reception would be, just showing up, but at least your friends out there took care of the awkwardness."

She had planned on talking to him; she had planned on some more ground rules. She had planned a better moment altogether, with her in something more flattering than her white coat and with him wearing... considerably less.

Because they had been having phone sex over the last week – but it was more than that. They had been intimate in other ways. Helen had told him how bored she was sometimes, sitting with her father, and how guilty she got when she was bored. Adam talked about almost drinking up all his father's beer and deciding that he probably shouldn't, and how old he felt compared to the other guys on the team now. They had given each other permission to be terrible, and it spilled over into uncontrollable guilty laughter, then whispered phone wanking. It was heady stuff, almost like being a teenager again, except this second adolescence was so much better than the first.

But over the phone was one thing. When he was in front of her, her resolutions to be sensible fled. In person, they couldn't afford to be hopped up on hormones. It wasn't that she couldn't control herself – of course she was in complete control of herself – she had just very deliberately decided that she was going to run her hands along the deeply muscled grooves of his abdomen and bury her mouth in his neck. She was going to let her fingers traverse his back. She was going to touch his elbows, his arms, the hard swells of his shoulders. She very deliberately stood on tiptoe and scraped her teeth on his chin. He seemed to enjoy it almost as much as she had.

In his presence, she had come to a few solid decisions and she felt good about them. Very good.

He smiled at her and pulled her up, his fingers delving into the woolly nap of her sensible black pants. And then he kissed her – they kissed each other – and she didn't even have the sense to kick herself for forgetting how dangerous this was. He lipped her delicately and her mouth opened and their tongues slid luxuriantly against each other. The insistent ache of her body bloomed and rippled until she wanted to starfish her arms and legs and mouth and leave everything open to him.

She might have said something like, *Unnnnhhh.*

They pulled apart.

"We shouldn't do this at your office," he said, in a rush.

"Good thinking," she mumbled. She stumbled back against the door, and he crushed her to it and started pulling off her white coat.

"What are you doing?"

"Taking this off so we can put on your outdoor clothing."

He slid his hands over her chest and waist and butt and kissed her again quickly and desperately.

She took another breath, a pause for consideration. They should talk, shouldn't they? Shouldn't they say something a little more substantial before they fell into bed? But it had been this way for them: Lead with the throbbing body parts, heavy as anchors, then accidentally throw the brain and heart into it. Because she could only delude herself so much; her heart was involved. How much, she couldn't – didn't want to – quite say.

Was that the involvement she wanted?

The decisions were coming faster and thicker. She wasn't sure she was giving them enough thought.

She had grabbed her jacket and was zipping it up, though. She stuffed her iPhone, her keys, and some papers into her bicycle bag. She looked around wildly to see if she'd missed anything. She would have to leave her bike at work. She would have to go to work the next morning in the same dirty clothing.

Who cares?

She pushed him out the door, flung a hasty good-bye at whatever body stood watching her, and only paused when she reached the sidewalk. If she seemed a little eager, it was because she was.

To be fair, sexual desperation was a little easier to deal with than the other stuff that they possibly were going to talk about.

They bumped their way down the street. It was the slowest walk in the world, partly because of perception, partly because they were both too turned on to walk very quickly.

"If you didn't want to finish in the office, you shouldn't have started anything," she grumbled.

"You're the one who leaned in."

"You're the one who brushed my boob."

At least the bickering was helping to move things along.

They pressed against each other in his elevator, his hands unzipping her jacket and pulling at her blouse, scrabbling underneath the cotton to find the soft skin at her waist and belly. She laughed a little bit, against his mouth. "Tickles," she murmured, and he made a sound between a laugh and a groan. "We should get dinner," he said, picking her up and pressing her against the wall of the elevator. "I should take you on some sort of date." A kiss on her neck. "I should hold out your chair and pay a guy to play the violin near you." A nip on her chin followed by a deep lick down her cleavage.

"I don't like violins," she managed to say, wrapping her legs firmly around his middle. "I am firmly against violins."

The elevator doors pinged open. Thank God no one was in the hallway. He hauled her out. "How about candles?" he murmured. Her blouse was completely open, and he was talking to the bare skin. "And flowers, tables full of flowers." He sucked her nipple through her bra, and she groaned. "So many huge flower arrangements that we can't really even talk over them, and we have to brush the foliage off our plates in order to eat," he said, the last part coming out in a gasp as she slid down his body and reached in his pants pocket.

She took creative license with looking for his keys.

"Theoretically, this is how you'd woo me? Like a sitcom character?" She reached around the front of his pants.

He kissed her again and grabbed the keys. Their bodies almost fell against the door. As it was, Adam let the momentum propel them gently onto the hallway floor. He tried to kick the door shut, while pawing her pants off and tangling himself in his coat. Helen began giggling helplessly. He paused to glare at her.

"A little help, please?"

She couldn't. She couldn't even get up. At the very least, she should shut the door, so that none of Adam's neighbors would see her lying on the floor with her jacket, blouse, and trousers open, her flesh spilling from the splits. Adam, back on his knees flailing wildly with his coat and shirt knotted around his arms, presented an equally undignified sight.

She writhed away from him on the floor and sprawled on her back, her arms wide open, laughter making her convulse helplessly. In the hilarity, she could feel the battle for her body. The zing of sexual frustration down her center tangled with pulses of almost hysterical giggles. He was almost helpless with it, too, which made it even harder for him to get out of his coat, and his bright laughing face looked so incredibly carefree that she wanted to get up and touch him, grab him, take handfuls of him, sink her teeth into his chest until she could taste the juices of his life. But instead, she launched herself on top of him, pushed him down, and put her knee on his chest, which only made him gasp harder. She clasped her hands and shook them in mock victory.

Then somehow, quite gracefully, he managed to release himself from his clothing and flip her onto her back again. By this time, one of them had managed to close the door, thank goodness. Because, judging by the gleam in his eye, what was likely to happen next shouldn't be shared with the neighbors.

The giggles were coming less rapidly now, just little sputters and quakes here and there, as he traced his finger over the bare stomach. His touch was so light, it should have tickled, but instead, she breathed shallowly and smoothed her hands down his chest. She had forgotten how golden and springy his hair was, how the light caught its glints so that his body gave off almost festive sparks.

"Happy New Year to me," she murmured.

"Happy New Year to us both," he said. "I'm really glad you're here."

She squeezed her eyes shut. "I'm really glad you're here, too," she whispered.

She couldn't say it while looking at him, with her voice strong. She meant it; she was so happy, and it was awful that one person could do that. It frightened her how much she meant it, how much he meant it. If she faced him, she would see it all – the lust, the sincerity, the pleasure, the happiness, the acceptance – in those pale, pale eyes.

So instead, she sat up and shrugged out of her blouse and jacket. He gazed at her bra, and she took advantage of his studiousness to pull his head down and run her fingers through his short, slippery hair. She kissed him as hard and deeply as she could. She could kiss him with earnestness and desire, she could pour everything she meant into her lips and frantic tongue, and he wouldn't see how vulnerable she was.

He pulled back with a gasp. "Helen, do you really want to do this on the floor? Because my knee…"

"No," she said.

She stood up and kicked off her shoes, pulling off her pants and underwear as she strode to the living room.

She bent herself over the back on the couch, her bare ass in the air, and gave him one hard glance.

His warm body pressed against her almost immediately, the hair of his legs rubbing against her calves, his erection heavy against the crease of her bottom. And suddenly everything was very serious.

"Fuck me," she said, gritting her teeth.

She was wet, the cool air making her even wetter, and the pressure of the solid couch against her would feel good once he started sliding into her. She braced her legs farther apart and grabbed one of the cushions on his couch, ready to bite into it. She tried not to squirm.

But instead of following orders, he bent over her and traced one curled finger down the back of her neck, down her spine, and palmed both of her cheeks with his warm hands.

He was murmuring something, but she couldn't quite hear him. So it was a surprise when he licked her, a thin firm line from the base of her neck, between her shoulder blades, down every nerve and bump in her spine. He crouched down between her legs to nose at her pussy, and she took the velveteen nap of the cushion in her teeth to gnash out a groan.

But his hands were parting her ass cheeks wider, pushing her up so she was nearly falling over onto the other side. His tongue was trying to reach her clit, his fingers pressed so hard into her bottom that they were bound to leave bruises. She gasped as he found her nub and began to suck, his hands kneading her bottom in rhythm, pulling everything taut as she bobbed her head up and down gasping and whimpering.

He pulled one hand down and used his fingers to twitch and tweak her clit. She curled her knees and tried to raise herself on her arms enough to look at him. He gave one taunting look to her and put his face down into her.

The sight of him there and the force of his tongue should have made her orgasm rush out. It should have spiked her body with sharp pangs of pleasure. She was breathless and aroused, but the tide of her happiness had carried her so high that she was suspended for a moment at the top, and it was as if she could see everything as it was about to crash. She could give it all up for him. He made her forget everything about herself, about the things that she needed to accomplish. He made her feel worthy, and that was frightening.

Of course, he'd always had that effect on her, but now she couldn't hang up the phone, she couldn't sneak out and walk away. Now there were feelings involved, and she had nowhere to put them. She felt him enter her in a heavy slide, and she cried out. It was startling, the jolt of impact rattling her teeth, as he took her. He had pulled her up again, his hands grasping her breasts, her hard nipples sliding between his fingers as he drove in again and again.

She was gasping with each impact, fighting herself not to get carried under. It wasn't bliss or pain, but something else equally powerful, completely illogical making her ride each of his thrusts, making her push back almost angrily, her legs braced wide and hard, feet flat on the floor as he thrust into her.

Some of the fury must have come through, because he stopped moving abruptly. "Helen," he said, his lips close to her ear, "am I hurting you?"

"No," she said, her voice cracking.

He pulled out of her, and she really did sob. Her strict stance deflated, and she let herself sag against the back of the couch.

His voice was strained, but he touched her back gently. "Helen, turn around."

She slumped over the couch, and she stayed limp as he pulled her up gently and turned her over.

He scanned her face. His breathing was labored.

She turned her face away and closed her eyes. After a moment, she felt him come near.

"I went too fast. Let's start all over," he said, and she felt his arms come under her as he picked her up.

He dropped her gently on the bed, and she felt him settle down beside her. "I'm all right. I just…" She buried her face in a pillow. "It would just be so easy to fall in love with you."

Oh *no*. She did not say that.

He took a moment before he spoke, and it was both reassuring and not. "It's scary for me, too."

Her hands still gripped the pillow. She couldn't look at him. So she kissed him again, letting some of the panic come through.

He gentled her with his hands and lips. Under the warmth of his mouth, she felt the tension come out of her. Almost reluctantly, she let go, her fingers uncurling, her body limp. He pulled away and kissed the soft skin inside her elbow, the top of her shoulder, her neck.

His eyes searched her face, a pair of lighthouse beams cutting through her fog. *It would be so easy*, she thought helplessly, as his body touched down gently over her skin. *It would be too easy.* Her hands came up, and she smoothed them over his shoulder blades, her thumbs digging deep into the grooves of muscle and bone. He was lipping her clavicles, her neck, and rubbing his cheek against hers. His eyes caught hers again, asking.

Or maybe it's easy because it's too late, she thought, as another tide of wanting engulfed her.

She nodded, and he slowly entered again. She clutched his shoulder and buried her face in his neck, but still, he continued to move inside her slowly. A wave rushed over her. She was drowning, drowning in him. She was just on the verge, so close, when he began to move faster as her body rolled again, twisting her like a damp cloth, and she felt herself fall.

Chapter Seventeen

"Are you really asleep?" he asked.

"No," she said, her voice muffled.

"Then I'm going to pick you up so I can pull the covers back."

She rolled over, and he lifted her and pulled back the sheets, inviting her in. Her hair fell around her face, and he stroked it back, tracing the line of her chin. They got under together, and she burrowed against him, her nose pressed against his chest. She still hadn't looked at him, so he lifted the sheet to stare at her quiet body.

He had left red marks on her hips and ass. Her shoulders and neck had abrasions, too. When they'd had phone sex, somehow he had forgotten about this, the scratch on the delicate skin of her upper arm, the red spot at the tip of her chin. There was something so specific and wonderful and terrible about the way he'd marked her up. On the phone, they would talk fucking and pussy and cunt and cock. She would tell him about using her teeth. But the reality of the tiny marks dotting her skin, the purpled bruises, the bites – this was what happened, what they had done. She was in his apartment, in his bed, and her eyes were still shut as if she were afraid to look at him after she'd completely given herself over. To him. She'd let him strip away the delicate membrane that protected her fears, and as much as he was fiercely glad to have done it, he now felt like he needed to stand watch. He was the one who had made her vulnerable, and now he had to keep her safe.

He felt an arrow of sympathy for her. It was hard for her to be this open, to tell him how she felt, to just let herself go and feel everything between them. Helen did not like to depend on anyone except herself. But her intensity, her need for him, that had been impossible to disguise. And his heart swelled to think of how much she cared. "Helen," he said gently.

Her chin bobbed. He smoothed her hair and he felt a dot of relief when she snuggled into his neck. He could feel his chest grow tight.

She laughed shakily against him and finally looked up. "I said... too much. It's not like I can be in a relationship right now, Adam. Not with you."

"It's not like I can either."

"Oh." She stopped and seemed to gather herself up. "Why, because you're always on the road, docking into new vaginas?"

"No, because I'm old fashioned and I won't have a job much longer and I need some sort of self-respect."

She frowned now. Any minute she would be alert. "But I... were you fired? I thought you guys won some games." She sat up. "Haven't you made millions as a sports star?"

"I wasn't fired, Helen. I'm glad you watched the games. And no, I haven't saved up millions because I've been helping out my family and I haven't been much of a star. I'm retiring at the end of the season, and I don't have a backup plan. I don't have my life together enough to be in a relationship. Even though, I guess we're in one."

Had he ever just put it all out there like that? Now he was the one who wanted to close his eyes and burrow under the sheets. He stopped speaking, pained at the admission of his failures, at always disappointing people, failing to make shots, failing to stay in the majors, failing to live up to his potential – pained, especially, at admitting this to her.

She sprang out of bed and groped around on the floor and pulled on a shirt, and he felt even sadder. "You're telling me about having your life together? You are plenty together enough for a relationship. Not that I want one. Except, why am I even having this conversation with you? Do you have no idea how amazing it is that you'll – you'll remember that I like Pop-Tarts and that you'll listen to me talk about my dad. That you keep your cool and answer me back. You're huge and strong, but you're so gentle. I don't know anyone like you."

"That doesn't change the fact that it's over for me."

"Your job is over – well, not yet, but you aren't your job. You are more than that – a lot more."

"This from the woman who hates my current career. It will be different. You'll probably end up making more money over the long term than me. Are you okay with that?"

She looked thunderous. "Is that what this is about? Some sort of social construct of dudehood? *Me earn big money!* Do you think I honestly care?"

God, they were fighting. He hated fighting. They both took long breaths.

After a moment, Helen said, "That was uncalled for. I'm sorry. For that matter, having a job hasn't made me happy or particularly worthy of anything—"

"Helen."

"No, let me finish. This whole thing about salaries, this isn't you. The reason I lov— like you is because you let me be as much as I am. You even seem to like that I can get obsessive and that I can be aggressive and loud and disorganized and make mistakes."

"But I still need to be something, to do something."

"You are more than you know, Adam. Is this why you are doing all this stuff for the team? Why are they sending you everywhere? Why are they making you do the media rounds if they're going to drop you? Are you doing this so you can play longer?"

She got up and searched around for her clothing, and he noticed that the fabric of the T-shirt she'd thrown on was clinging to her thighs and ass as she groped around on the floor. The shirt was his.

"I'm not doing this so I can play longer. Yevgeny is interested in having me in his organization, and he sort of wants me to prove myself."

"In his organization as what?" she said.

He'd been given a temporary lift by seeing her in his tee. Now he felt his mood ebb again. "Well, he didn't exactly say."

"You're a good spokesperson for the team," Helen said slowly. "I can see why he'd want you to represent the Wolves. But I don't know, Yevgeny Molotov? You know what they say about him. That he has a personal eyebrow wrangler? That he only hires assistants he can sleep with, for dual usage. That he keeps a 182-room mansion stocked with blondes, brunettes, redheads, and whatever you call women with black hair? Why isn't there a name for women with black hair? Or is it better that we don't have one so that they aren't like products?"

Adam tried to decide which question to answer first. He decided to choose the easier one.

"So, you're saying that you're offended he didn't choose you for one of the rooms?"

"No, I'm saying that all signs point to the fact that he treats people like spare parts. And like I said, you are—"

"More, I get it. You really think the lady-house rumor is true?"

She frowned. "No. Yes. I just think it's telling that those are the kinds of thing people say about him. It's not that surprising. If you get to that level in business, you probably do count people as capital. But this isn't really about Molotov. I mean, it's more about you. I'm just concerned that you're just going to accept whatever crap job he decides to give you now so that in the future, he can give you another crap job to do because you don't understand how much you're worth."

Well, what else was a guy going to do?

"I can hold my own against Molotov," he said.

But maybe Helen was right. It was funny, in those first years, when he was still a hotshot player, Adam would have laughed at Molotov, coming to a party with his stupid bodyguards. Adam thought he was a big shot then. But he'd failed before — failed hard enough that he was no longer sure precisely what he was worth. And that doubt had colored his dealings in subsequent years.

Damn it.

"Listen, it's not about holding your own and going toe to toe and all that masculine crap," Helen said. "I can understand how hard it is to remake yourself. I had to when I was a teenager, and yes, I say it's a relief now and that I'm happy now. But at the time, it was horrible. And I had to do a lot of thinking before I realized that I wasn't limited. That I was free to figure out what I wanted to do — as long as I knew that it wouldn't be what I was doing before. And it won't be the same."

"You're happy now? That's rich."

It came out far more bitter than he meant it to, but instead of slapping him upside the head, Helen looked at him and pursed her lips. She might have been trying to hide a smile. "Maybe you're right, but I'm not arguing with you while you're hungry and naked," she said, prowling out of the bedroom. "Let's get takeout before you really start fixing for a fight."

"Oh, I'm the one who's fixing for a fight?" he asked, trailing after her. "You started it."

Still, she wasn't wearing underwear. And really, she should never, ever do that.

Thirty minutes later, Adam took a careful bite of chicken tikka masala.

"Is Yevgeny Molotov even this guy's real name?" she asked. "It sounds made up. I'll bet he's not even Russian. His name is probably Stewart Klunk. He's probably from Boise."

It was a relatively primitive strategy she was employing. Distract the defensemen with noise and fancy stickwork. *Please.* He wasn't Hall of Fame material, but he was entirely capable of dealing with that ruse. He was going to let her ride it out.

"Does his Russian accent sound real and overdone? Does he sort of play it up and do very stereotypical things, like drink vodka?"

"He claims he was the accent coach for Sean Connery in *The Hunt for Red October.*"

Helen snorted. "I bet he has a caviar wench, someone who has to lie on the table while he eats it off of her with a tiny, tiny spoon."

"Oh yeah, I was at that party."

"Shut up! You were not!"

And then she looked down. And in that split second, he felt himself losing her again. "Helen, it's your turn. What's going on?"

"This whole thing scares me," she said.

"Obviously. And you're trying to scare me, too."

"Yeah."

"And you're sort of trying to regain a sense of control by jabbing at me."

"Yep."

She chewed slowly. "I guess I just don't want to clarify things," she said. "I like it a little amorphous and ambiguous. I mean, why can't we go on as we are, just talking and having sex and never ever leaving this apartment and eating Indian food for the rest of our lives."

"You aren't actually eating much of it."

"It's supposed to last for the rest of our lives. Weren't you paying attention?"

"A lesser man would point out that you just asked to move in with me."

She swallowed and took a sip of water. "What I mean is, things are good here; they're great, actually. But as soon as we go out into the real world again, I'm me and you're you and bad things will inevitably happen."

"What bad things?"

"This could break my heart." She hurried on. "Molotov wants you to be the public face of the pro-arena, pro–brain injury deal. That puts us on different sides."

"I think that part of the PR plays on our chemistry, though."

"Please, I barely made an impact in the news. And I just don't want to be part of it. My life is complicated enough already. In a way, those stupid radio and TV shows were good. It showed me I really didn't want to be attracting the wrong side – I don't want to become a photo op for the hospital chair and her slimy husband. I don't want to be beaned by a bat at a softball game. I don't want to be photographed in a pink baseball cap. So if we're going to be together, I want you to keep me out of it. This has to remain a secret."

He'd had just about enough. He stood up and picked her up.

He carried her to the bedroom. He dropped her on the bed, stripped the T-shirt off and threw it into a corner, and just stood looking at her. Her eyes were big and round, but after a brief pause, she managed to keep talking. "It's not as if we're totally sneaking around. My friends already probably know. I mean, I don't think Sarah's going to be able to keep her mouth shut about your appearance in the office."

He stripped off his boxers and was pleased at the way her eyes sharpened, even as her mouth softened. She straightened slowly, her attention fixed on him, and as her neck stretched up slowly, one hand slid up to caress her shoulder, her collarbones.

"We can keep it quiet," he said, gruffly. "We don't have to give each other pet names. But it makes a difference to me for you to say that we are together. And it makes a difference to you, otherwise you wouldn't be making such a big deal about it. Whether you like to admit it or not, I mean something to you and you mean something to me. I want to think of you in my bed, in my life. I want you to miss me when I'm gone, and when I'm gone, I want to talk with you on the phone and make you come and listen to you moan in my ear. In the world beyond this city, I don't think anyone cares about this little campaign or the arena that Molotov built. We're not going to get hung up on Portland problems."

"Portland problems?" she said, her eyes eating him up.

Her hand drifted up, and her fingers pulled gently and absently on the coarse hair on his thighs, each little tug making his balls heavy. If he and Helen were so out of sync, how could she do this to him, almost lazily, almost carelessly. How could he feel this much?

"Portland problems. You know, people who want reusable panic attack bags with all the comforting crinkle of brown paper. Or people who want to set the worms in their vermicomposter free. Declan Quail." He stretched down beside her, and she brought him close. "No one else anywhere cares about this stuff. Portland problems. And we aren't going to let Portland problems drive us apart."

Her voice was husky. "I'm surprised you know what a vermicomposter is. Living here has turned you into a dirty hippie."

"Very dirty."

Her hand went behind him to squeeze his ass. She gazed at where their bodies were pressed together. She looked a little sad — or maybe it was the way her mouth was turned down. But when she glanced up, her eyes were full of mischief.

"I want this," she said. She rolled her hips and kissed him until he couldn't stand it anymore. "I want to be with you. But I don't know what it is and maybe I should."

He didn't know whether to be gratified or annoyed. But at least it was some sort of relationship. So instead, he just took her to bed again.

–

She left again early in the morning. This time, at least she'd warned him that she would. She told him that she had morning rounds, but it didn't make him less disappointed to find himself amorously entwined with a pillow instead of with her.

To be fair, the pillow was very soft. But the timing sucked. He'd be gone again this week, and soon, the state legislature would vote on the arena.

As he stalked to the shower, he consoled himself with the fact that at least she promised she would be there when he came back. There would be more dinners, more nights, more arguments, more admiration of the smooth workings of her legs and thighs, more lips and licking and sucking and kissing.

The shower was not cold enough.

Her skittishness hurt, just a little bit. He wanted to make her forget, to make her stop thinking, and to make her think that he was entirely worth forgetting everything for. But then, she wouldn't be Helen.

It also worried him. Because if she was hesitant now, how would she really feel when this season was over and he was no longer playing hockey? She said she didn't care about money, and she even hated that he was always getting knocked around for his job. But when he just became a big, unemployed lunk, then what would happen to them? He was happy to be the calm one in the face of her energy. He enjoyed her brain and her mouth. But that was because their footing, if not equal, had a give and take to it that seemed natural even when they were arguing. What happened when that changed, when he changed? Would he retreat completely? Would she expect him to cook meals, keep a spotless apartment? Would he have an apartment to live in? What if one day she wanted him out? Why was he being weird and sexist all of a sudden? It was going to be different.

He'd hoped that she would be there in Portland in summertime, that he would be holding hands with her and walking along the path next to the river. He could imagine sunshine and life. He wanted it with her. He wanted it so badly that his stomach hurt.

He had no choice if he wanted what he had with Helen to stay the same. He had to keep this thing with Yevgeny Molotov. And if he was on Molotov's side now, then he had to stay away, at least in public, from her.

They would have to sneak around so that they could be together later. The image of Helen, clad in black leather, emerging from the shadows to fling herself at him, was enormously appealing. So was the idea of simply shutting themselves in his bedroom for days at a time to have sex.

Still, after he showered, he went to his computer to check his e-mail. He'd tried contacting old professors and former coaches for references for graduate programs in psychology and education that he'd begun applying to.

It had been a long time since he'd been in a classroom, and while he hadn't been a failure the first time around, he hadn't been stellar. Finding most of his old teachers hadn't responded, he started to jot down notes to define what he had with Yevgeny Molotov. Helen was right – Molotov could jerk him around, if he wasn't careful. He needed something more solid. He needed something on paper. He needed something that Helen would approve of.

After all, how was she supposed to respect him when he felt like he couldn't respect himself?

–

She hadn't been kidding last night when she'd told him she wanted to stay locked away with Indian food and his naked self – she had wanted to stay in his apartment forever and never leave. And he would've let her. He'd be happy about it.

Wasn't that frightening?

Instead, she left Adam's warm bed way too early that morning again. The rounds and notes and paperwork she completed bleary-eyed were little consolation for leaving. His bed was great, too, a real grown-up's bed. It was huge – she supposed it had to be to hold his very large, very densely muscled, very grown-up body. His sheets were always crisp, too. And, well, there was Adam, and his warm arms and his perfect broad back and his strong, round ass. She wished she could loll around with him longer.

To make up for her laziness, she scoured the latest research extra attentively that evening. She uncovered a new monograph about a treatment for essential tremor in Parkinson's. A small European company was taking the drug to phase-two safety trials. She cross-checked the drug and found that it had been approved for use in Canada to treat – of all things – reflux. A heartburn drug was the best lead she'd found after months of looking.

If she could convince her father's physician to prescribe it off-label, then maybe it would help.

She settled into her desk chair as she set out to research. She was on call for the rest of the night, but Adam was leaving for a few games on the road.

She was trying not to make a big deal about the fact that she would feel out of sorts when he was gone – that she missed him now – because making a big deal meant that she cared. She was already trying not to think about the fact that he occupied a space in her brain during her day, silent and submerged like a massive creature of the deep whose slightest movements could send ripples everywhere. But it was hard to forget he was there, quiet as he was. This morning, as she came out of the bathroom, she turned around to see him give her pillow a delicate, wistful stroke, as if she still lay there. He had thought she'd already left. She saw his eyes blaze to life as he realized that she hadn't yet gone, and she felt a zing from her stomach, deep down to her heels. How could she not respond to that? How could she feel nothing? Later, when she really had left, he'd fallen asleep again and he was gripping that same pillow, his face pressed into it as if he needed to breathe her scent.

How was it that a part of her was already planning for the moment when he stopped playing, when he'd be able to sleep in with her, when they would sit in the grass somewhere with their shoes off, happy and relaxed. She could be lulled into seeing a future with him. She could be so happy.

Or was that some sort of illusion, too?

Her phone rang and she started.

It was her mother.

Helen's heart sank. "What's wrong?" she asked. "How is he?"

Damn it, she'd only gotten one stupid lead on one drug and already—

"He's fine, Helen. He's fine."

"Oh." *Oh.* "Good."

She got up slowly. Her knees felt creaky, and her eyelids abraded her vision. She glanced at the clock. How long had she been sitting?

"We found a buyer for the house," May Yin said.

It was not what Helen expected at all. It had hardly been on the market. "It's the new doctor and her family," May Yin explained. "They have a young son and daughter, just like we did. I talked to Dr. Rajpul on the phone. She wanted to know what the community was like, if it was welcoming."

"And what did you tell her?"

"I told her people's attitudes and tolerance had changed a lot from when I started there," May Yin said firmly.

"And then she wanted to know about dance lessons for her daughter, and I told her about you."

Her mother prattled on, sounding proud and happy. She was furnishing her new apartment in Vancouver and planning to visit her sister in Victoria. Helen realized, guiltily, that May Yin hadn't been able to do that for a while. When was the last time she'd been able to leave her husband alone for more than a couple of hours? Even when home help came to help bathe Harry or prepare a meal, May Yin was tethered to the house. Of course, Helen had known that it wasn't just about needing more help with dusting and sweeping and ferrying Harry to appointments. May Yin had to keep track of him during the night. She had to make sure he didn't wander.

All of which Helen knew, intellectually, from working in the field.

But when it came to her own parents – when it came to her childhood – she had a blind spot about how things operated.

Maybe it hadn't been as idyllic as she'd once imagined it was, all lush green apple orchards and townspeople who knew each other. And it wasn't as harsh as her brother remembered it – although his memories were no doubt darker than hers. Her experience was different from her brother's and it was different from her mother's, and it would probably have been different had she been the same person in a different time. Her home was gone, but it had never really been there. Her life was here in Portland now.

With Adam.

"Mom, you've done a lot of work, and I wanted to say thank you for always being there," she said quickly, almost trying to slip it in, almost hoping that her mother wouldn't understand the mumbled phrase.

May Yin paused. "It's my job," she said, almost gently.

There was a long silence, and Helen understood that her mother knew what she was trying to say.

She took a deep breath.

Now would probably be a good time to bring up the lead on the drug she'd found. They could talk about how her dad was doing on his new treatment plan, if he was sleeping, if he was eating. But that wasn't what they needed to do. For now, this moment was for them.

"Maybe I can come up next month," she said instead. "Visit your new apartment and just hang out?"

Chapter Eighteen

Adam got back home from his road trip late in the night and was up early for a morning show appearance. He half hoped Helen would be at the apartment waiting for him when he arrived so that he would get to savor one moment with her, even if she were just asleep in his bed. But she was working early in the morning, and Janel had stepped up his schedule, gearing up for the anti-arena rally this weekend and the upcoming vote. And – almost as an afterthought – he had a game tonight.

He wouldn't have a moment from the time his alarm went off. So he didn't leave a key for her, he didn't ask her to come over, and he tried not to think of how far away she felt, even though they were in the same city for the first time in a week.

Meanwhile, on the way to the morning show, Janel was giving him notes on his appearance. She told him to lose the suits, to be more animated, but not to shout. She wanted him to smile more. She said he should grow out his hair, and he reminded her that there wasn't that much time before the vote. She wanted him to be around her a lot more than he wanted.

He usually listened to about half of the things that Janel told him to do. To distract her from the other half, he usually sent Serge to flirt with her, and that worked fairly well. Too bad he wasn't here. Adam closed his eyes, but Janel seemed to pick up on his thoughts. "His accent is so cute," she was musing. "It's too bad it would sound terrible on TV. Otherwise, he'd be great."

"His accent is hardly noticeable," Adam said. "Or do microphones add ten pounds to his tongue?"

Janel rolled her eyes at him. "Americans don't like accents," she said.

"You like him."

"Well, I'm more worldly," Janel said.

Somehow, despite the power boots and the lipstick and the smartphone, he highly doubted that. Whenever she said Yevgeny's name, she sighed like an old mattress. And when she got a text from him, or more likely, one of his assistants, she jabbed at her phone so eagerly that he feared for its delicate carapace. She clearly liked accents more than she knew.

She romanticized Yevgeny, and that worried Adam a little bit. Despite her bossiness and her nosiness, and the fact that he knew that she was feeding information into the Molotov grid, he'd started feeling brotherly toward her. That's how little sisters were, after all, always tagging along, always in your business.

He nodded absently as Janel continued to talk, and he dozed the rest of the way in the car.

Tonight after the press and the practice and the game, he'd see Helen, he thought.

He fake-smiled his way through the morning show. He grimaced through training and through a series of nutritionally balanced meals. Janel had brought in photographers to document a day in the life of the Wolves.

At last, the day was almost over. All he had to do was get through this stupid evening and another gauntlet of postgame press. They were just filing out of the room after looking at some game tape, when Serge nudged him. "Your girlfriend is waiting for you," Serge said.

Adam whipped his head up. Helen was here in the practice facility? But of course, Serge meant Janel again who was hovering at the door, tapping furiously at her phone, no doubt with another list of tasks for him.

"*She's* definitely not my girlfriend," Adam said.

"Why not? After Dr. Frobisher proved too difficult, I thought you'd like someone peppier."

"Janel's peppy like a nursery school teacher, and she treats me like a toddler."

He *was* as grumpy as a two-year-old who'd just woken from a nap. From here, he could see that Janel looked excited. She kept glancing at her phone and pacing. When he approached, she practically leaped into the air, as if electrified.

Great.

She grabbed him, pulling him through the halls and outside into the crisp Portland air. A huge Hummer limo waited for them. It was black, for discretion, Adam supposed.

Janel was practically dancing. She paused only to let Adam help her into the monster vehicle, and she was glowing with happiness by the time he clambered inside.

Yevgeny Molotov was sprawled back against the middle seat. His bodyguard was scrunched into a corner. The rest of the entourage was scattered over the rest of the Hummer. If they weren't staring at smartphones, they were staring at Molotov. There were a lot of people. Maybe the Hummer was practical, after all. "Adam," he said, not bothering to offer his hand. "Thanks for agreeing to meet me. Would you care for a Perrier or perhaps a Fresca?"

He motioned at Janel with two fingers. She presented Adam with a bottle as if she were a sommelier. Adam shook his head.

What was it about men like him, Adam wondered, not for the first time. Janel was glowing. Every bit of attention Molotov gave her made her open wider and turn, like a sunflower following the light. Money probably helped, although Adam wasn't cynical enough to believe that it was everything. The illusion of power was probably a big part of it. The confidence. The grooming, the expensive suits.

But was it just that, or did Molotov just have some sort of ineffable quality? Some vitality, some life spark, or even some dark gloriousness that made people glom to him like peanuts to caramel? Okay, so he was good looking in a louche European way, the kind of good looking that could slide into weediness, potbellies, and comb overs late in life. Janel laughed at all of Molotov's jokes, but as far as Adam could tell, though, Molotov wasn't particularly witty. Did he just have a giant dick? If acting like one were a true indication of size, then, probably, yes.

Or maybe it was a certain type of woman who flocked to Molotov. Or a certain type that Molotov allowed to surround him. Janel seemed made of sturdier stuff, but then...

He wondered how Helen would fare against the billionaire. Would she be starstruck? He didn't think so, but they would never *ever* meet, Adam decided. He should at least spare her that.

"What brings you to Portland, Yevgeny?"

"I'm here to see some hockey," Yevgeny said, matching his tone.

"We'd like you to step up your campaign for the final push. We've been doing quite well," Janel interjected as she pulled an iPad out of her purse. The case, Adam noted, matched the one for her iPhone. "The sports blog HeavyRinker.com had an in-depth look at the team's roster yesterday and didn't once mention the arena. The sports call-in shows have been concentrating on the new players, and you, of course. The wins have been helping."

Yevgeny looked a little bored. Adam wondered if they'd bothered glancing at the document he'd e-mailed them earlier this week.

"The arena is going before the state legislature Wednesday, so we're going to have you write a few more blog posts and do more interviews. There's also a rally scheduled in Portland this weekend."

Yevgeny closed his eyes. "Too bad we can't dig up that little doctor again. Where has she been hiding? Janel, do you think we could arrange that? Have Adam meet her somewhere public where there's a lot of press?" He waved his hand dismissively. "If you can make her cry, Adam, I'll give you another little bonus."

"Intimidation is my job on ice, but it's not what I do in real life," Adam said sharply. "I don't think it's good PR to make a person cry, and I certainly don't want to confront someone in public."

"Come on, where is your sense of sport, Adam? What if I sweeten the pot? I'll let you have a go at Janel here. Or maybe one of the other women in the organization."

Janel sucked in a breath, and Adam felt his stomach turn. "That is—" he began.

But Janel cut him off. "Yevgeny, sit back and be quiet."

There was a moment of silence in the Hummer.

Amazingly, Yevgeny did seem to retreat in face of Janel's justified fury. It was very clear how Janel had risen through the ranks. Underneath all the nice was steel. When she spoke again, her voice was low. "Crap like this is exactly why you hired me, and crap like this is also why you don't get to be the face of the organization here. You need to get some respect for your people and fast. As for you, Adam, I never thought I'd have to say this, but you unclench that fist and calm down right now. He's using me to yank your chain."

She was right. He was ready to punch the man.

Molotov looked smug. He'd done it on purpose – although who he was trying to rattle, Adam wasn't sure. Adam tried to relax and found that it wasn't really working. "How can you work for him when he says stuff like that?"

"I refuse to be a pawn for him forever," Janel said, steel in her voice. "Yevgeny, we need to stop wasting time and get down to business."

Yevgeny wrinkled his nose. "All my employees are spiky today," he said, mock-petulantly.

Adam felt another wave of helpless fury wash over him. He didn't know how Janel was managing to ignore her boss's needling.

"We're prepping the final push of a major PR campaign. I wanted you both here to talk about the document you sent over last week."

"Adam's little demands," Yevgeny said.

"If they're little, then I'm sure you won't have trouble accommodating them," Adam said.

"The team has won a few games. They're getting some attention. That doesn't put you in a position to ask for money or a title. All you Americans are alike. Your reputation is business, business, business, but when it comes to money, you want it all on paper. And then, then when it's finally all written down, you don't want to sign anything until you get your sister and brother and grandmother to read it. In other countries, the men I usually deal with say, 'I'm going to give you two million dollars and a Siberian tiger,' and they shake your hand, and the deal is closed. No zoning permits, no plumbing permits, no naive concerns over things like sanitation or adequate ventilation or child labor laws. Children need to learn early that life is very difficult." Molotov jabbed the air with a manicured finger. "They need skills, like masonry and roofing. The next day, you have a new building and the hosts have invited you to have tiger barbecue. Done. Done."

"Adam has been doing interviews. We've had him write a few press releases because he's actually pretty good at it. Asking for a title and compensation for this work might be unorthodox, but it's fair," Janel snapped. "And this isn't all on Adam. You have to be better at this, too, Yevgeny. You have to be better overall. That remark earlier, that was uncalled for. You're alienating me, your staff, and the people who are supposed to endear you to Portlanders. You are your own worst enemy."

Adam hooked a glance over at her. She was again the only person of color and the only woman trapped in a stupid vehicle with a bunch of white men who were being assholes.

And although he wanted to smash Molotov's smug face, he needed to step back and take his cues from Janel. It was not his place, and it wasn't his battle. Or so Janel had indicated.

Adam took a deep breath. He thought of Helen and his hopes for the future and tried to strive for a reasonable tone. "Listen, I've worked hard for the last couple of months. Yes, I'm representing the team and that's part of the deal, it's part of my existing playing contract. My point is we had talked about this before, and I want some of my experience acknowledged. We've had some tangible success. People actually know who the team is. We've seen an uptick in sales. We've seen some change in opinion."

"What makes you think it's due to you?"

"If you thought it wasn't working, you wouldn't be here meeting with me," Adam said.

"Janel made me." Molotov closed his eyes. "Titles are not important at Molotov International."

"Humor us."

Molotov closed his eyes. Twitching one finger in Janel's direction, he said, "Fine. Make him an assistant in charge of special projects for the Portland Wolves or whatever it is Adam suggested—"

"*Oregon* Wolves," Adam said.

Yevgeny ignored him. "Reporting to you, Janel. He's your responsibility. We don't need to see each other again."

"And I wanted my bonus doubled."

Yevgeny waggled his finger Adam-ward and said, "You can take it up with Janel."

Janel gave Adam a terse nod.

Adam resisted his violent urge to pry Yevgeny's eyes open. And at this moment, he hated his team, his organization, and most of all himself. But instead of doing anything about it, he opened the door and slid out of the vehicle. "Thanks, Janel," he said with no real warmth in his voice.

To Molotov, he said nothing.

–

It was her first live professional game! In fact, it was the first time she'd ever been to the Rose Quarter. The arena wasn't full – but Helen could feel the energy, an energy that she never sensed when she watched on television.

Okay, so sometimes she watched the games on mute, so that she could study the impacts without the announcers jabbering.

Petra and Sarah had teased Helen mercilessly about seeing Adam play when she asked them to go to the Wolves game with her. Luckily, Petra's mom was in town, so Helen was spared another round of bad hockey puns. But Sarah was there with homemade snacks. She was already crunching on dried chickpeas. Helen wanted a hot dog, but she grabbed a few red pepper strips from Sarah's Ziploc bag.

She chewed nervously, thinking of what kinds of things she'd tell Adam afterward. "Nice punching!" was probably not something she'd be able to say to him.

And who knew if there would be any punching, anyway?

She grabbed the bag from Sarah's hand. "Hey," Sarah said, making no move to take the bag. "Bring your own snacks." Sarah was scanning the ice. "Why are you so antsy?"

"What if I don't like the game?"

"You don't like it already. Nothing changes."

"What if—?"

Sarah sighed. "Think of it this way: You've already gotten your most fundamental incompatibilities out of the

246

way – and in public, too. Now there's nothing left but sparkles and orgasms. You like him – a lot. I've never seen you that way with anyone before. And he looks at you like you're a lake and he's parched."

"It's not like you to be so optimistic and laissez faire."

"I'm turning over a new leaf."

"He doesn't even know I'm here."

"If he knew you were here, he would've gotten us better seats. Maybe a private viewing booth with snacks."

"You wouldn't eat them anyway."

"Maybe there'd be a handsome man holding a tray. In an ideal world, that's what handsome men would always be doing – holding out trays, asking if you were satisfied."

They stood for the national anthems. Sarah knew the words to "O Canada" and the "Star Spangled Banner," and she sang them vigorously. Helen couldn't remember either. Then they sat down.

The good thing about being there live was that she could yell and other people were yelling with her. When Adam came up, she whooped and she was happy to see that everyone else did, too. The bad thing was that she couldn't really see his face.

The puck dropped and he wasn't playing yet, so she let her attention drift to the things she didn't usually pay attention to on television. The sharp rapping sounds of blades and sticks. The smell of the ice. The players' graceful turns as they skated around to watch the puck. In ballet, they had tried to move as coolly and smoothly across the floor as they could. In hockey, they actually could glide, and Helen felt a little jealous of how graceful it looked. She laughed softly to herself. She'd told herself to watch the game the way Sarah was: hunched over and almost angry. Instead, she found herself focusing on minutiae.

Maybe that was enough. She winced when Adam accused her of hating his job. But could she deny his words? Sarah was wrong: She and Adam hadn't gotten their fundamental incompatibilities out of the way. They knew what they were, yes, but just because they tussled and argued and had sex afterward didn't mean that talking would make their mismatch go away.

Midway through the second period, Adam shot onto the ice. Helen took a deep breath and almost couldn't let it out. He was... angry? He practically radiated with energy. As he hurtled toward another player, his movements seemed bigger and, well, more furious than she was used to. She blinked. Was it because she was watching it live? Did television somehow blur the sharper movements?

Then he made his first hit.

WHUMP! He went hard, skating right into the guy, and she wasn't even sure why. Sarah yelled something garbled beside her, but she couldn't even turn and respond. What had the guy done? Had he said something? Did she just not understand hockey? She felt the first tick in her head as she started counting the hits he made – as she always did.

The crowd was screaming now. Skinny hipsters in layers and layers of ironic T-shirts, out for blood. And

Adam was out there cutting across lines, skating hard. His clothes were loose and sloppy, but she could almost imagine spikes of rage protruding under his jersey.

Sarah leapt up. "We scored!" she yelled at Helen.

Helen rose and looked at the big screen. The camera focused on the center, who had a grim smile on his face. His teammates were patting him on the back. But Helen's eyes went back to the ice where Adam skated in short angry sweeps, seemingly not caring. He really was furious at something.

Why is he angry?

He'd been tired over the last week on the phone, his voice gravelly with fatigue. But there hadn't been any urgency – well, not the livid kind. And Adam right now looked really, really tense.

His cheekbone ticked, and she could imagine a drop of perspiration sliding down its sculpted surface.

Again – WHUMP! – this time from behind. The big guy from the other team smashed right into Adam. His helmet bounced right against the boards. She could feel it almost rattling her own teeth even though the crowd was screaming. She tensed her jaw until there was probably a tic there, as pronounced as his.

But instead of fighting, he left the ice. He was wiping his face, and she saw a little blood on the ice before his teammates skated over it and made it a faint pink smear.

"Breathe in through the nose, out through the mouth," Sarah said, her voice authoritative and cool.

Helen felt Sarah's hand at her back.

"I'm not having a panic attack."

"You're not, but maybe we shouldn't watch the rest of this."

"You're enjoying yourself."

"I'm not going to enjoy myself if I have to scrape you off the icky floor. Ugh. Maybe we *should* get a new arena. This one will never be clean."

Helen felt herself laugh.

"That's better," Sarah said. "Look, your boy is fine. He's back on the ice. He'll probably get a bonus or a fatter contract out of his performance."

"He will?"

"Yeah. Not that I follow hockey, but people are talking about him. Talking enough that even I've heard something."

He was swooping back around the ice, smooth and graceful despite being slammed and hit. She let out a cold, long breath, and she felt it for the first time. Pride. Mixed in with all the fear was a hard, resilient knot of pride that pushed so hard against her chest that it almost made her want to burst into laughter or tears. She was proud of him, of his strength and his power, which she could finally see unleashed. And her pride worried her, because that meant that she was changing, that she could see why he brought on the violence, the blood, the mayhem that he could cause.

The acknowledgment was seeping through her system, anesthetizing her fingers and slowing her heart; she could see him, for the first time. He wasn't just the man who shared her bed or her opponent or a subject of study. He was an athlete, someone great, something magnificent and wonderful. Not that she hadn't thought he was great and wonderful and magnificent before, but she had never thought about it when it came to Adam and hockey. She hadn't thought of him as an athlete, maybe because he had always been self-effacing. He didn't know his worth. All along, he had been incredible in ways she could barely wrap her mind around, and he didn't know it.

But all of that just made it harder to think about the ways she could lose – had maybe already lost – him if he kept doing this. Watching him be great was making her hurt.

He had an assist shortly before the end of the period. She was glaring at him so hard that she wasn't watching the puck. All she saw was the sharp snap of his stick back and that split second pause as he followed its path. She saw the swirl he made when it went in the goal and the stream of teammates thumping him on the back.

But someone on the other team must have said something, because Adam was turning and yelling something at the biggest guy on the team. In another minute, they were circling each other, and before Helen had time to close her eyes and shield her open, aching heart, the fists were flying.

Chapter Nineteen

At least he didn't end up in the hospital. He wouldn't have known what to say to Helen if he showed up there looking like he did now.

It had been the most brutal fight he'd had in years. At the beginning of the period, the Calgary center had bumped his shoulder. Adam had elbowed him, as a matter of course. Then later, the center, who had already pushed Adam before, said something like, *Asshole*. Maybe *Asshat*, possibly *Asswipe*, and then the gloves were off, and both teams were a bloody pile mash in the middle of the ice.

So now he sported a cut on his lip, a rapidly swelling eye, and a bruise on his cheekbone. His face and shoulder felt raw. His ribs hurt; his knee hurt like hell. When he'd staggered off the ice, he'd been tempted to hurl his gloves into the stands and give them all the finger. He'd thought it, but he didn't have the energy to do that.

Now he was out for the next few games. He'd gotten off easy.

In retrospect, he had been keyed up enough to really whale on someone and the other team had known it. After that Hummer talk with Yevgeny, he'd still had all that excess anger and holding it in hadn't helped him.

He'd been mobbed by reporters afterward, too. "What triggered the incident?" "What's the extent of your injuries?" "Are you going to protest the suspension?" "Do you feel like you've come back?" "Do you think you'll be suspended?" they yelled.

Janel was somewhere at the back, probably tweeting his responses or just making crap up.

Someone thrust a microphone in his face. It's possible that he might have snarled. He didn't remember what he said. He was exhausted, and he bundled himself into a car and plodded home as soon as possible. He was supposed to see Helen, but he felt uneasy. His whole aching, sore, tender body throbbed for her. But although his wounds were mostly superficial, he knew he looked terrible. Worse, he'd let himself get too angry. His rage had been a red line of focus that kept him hard and furious until at last he'd snapped. He'd probably looked good on the ice, but it didn't make him feel good.

She was a doctor; she was used to growly patients with wounds. Right?

At least he was home, he thought, finally stretching out on his bed with gel packs dotting his body – correction: stretched out on his side of the bed. Helen wasn't there yet.

He checked his phone and, of course, found a picture of himself, battered, bloody, and ugly, on the front page of the ESPN website. "Howling Mad," the headline read. He continued to scan the article dispassionately. They had ended up winning. The comments were bloodthirsty.

Some people wanted to stop his violence with violence. Some people thought he hadn't hit hard enough. The Wolves were finally showing their mettle after some growing pains, the story read.

He was described in *Rinky Business* as the *de facto* team leader, an eloquent goon. They also unearthed an old publicity photo of him shirtless from his rookie year. Was he supposed to be flattered?

He was happy they'd won, of course, but he hoped Helen hadn't watched this particular game.

His phone rang. *Helen.* He sucked in a breath.

"I'm downstairs. Let me up," she said, without preamble.

"Are you sure? I'm tired. I can't be your stud boy tonight."

She snorted. "Tough luck. You haven't given it to me in a week or more."

Jesus. He'd been joking – but it appeared there was an interested party in his pants. Her voice and her rough words were enough. His head fell back against the bed with a thunk. He rose and went to push the release to let her upstairs. Then he braced himself for his happiness and her unhappiness.

–

Just how hurt is he?

Helen willed her tension down as she rode the elevator to his apartment. After all, Adam hadn't been admitted to hospital. She'd checked. He'd sounded fine on the phone – a little nasal, a little tired. But he had his wits.

The elevator doors slid open, and she looked down to notice that her fingers had gripped the handrail so hard that red lines crossed her skin.

The door was cracked open for her, and she stretched a smile across her face in preparation for him. And there he was – standing, at least, leaning in the door frame, shirtless and bruised, his eye swollen shut. And he was trying to smile at her with cracked lips.

He was fine. Everything would heal. It looked ugly, but the wounds were superficial. She should have been ecstatic, but a sob threatened to escape her throat. She wanted to grab him and absorb all of his wounds into her body, to make him whole. But of course, she swallowed her warring impulses down and tried to look at him with the detachment of a physician.

But she wasn't his doctor.

He moved toward her and hesitantly put his arms around her. He was a little damp, but he felt warm and wonderful. *He's hurt*, she reminded herself. *Don't sink into him.* She gave him a quick kiss on the cheek – the uninjured one – and slipped away from him to close the door. She knew that he could feel her distance.

"You should be in bed," she said after a moment.

Adam leaned into her again, as if asking her to take his weight, then pulled her in and kissed her. Hard. She couldn't help herself. She opened her mouth and moved closer and grasped him, her fingers moving greedily over the warm muscles of his back.

256

And then she tasted the blood of his split lip in her mouth, and she remembered.

She pulled back almost in a panic. "You need to get back to bed, now," she said.

He blotted his mouth with a tissue. "Like I said, I can't be your stud boy tonight."

"Drop it," she said, grimly steering him toward his bedroom.

She took off her jacket, draped it on a chair, and motioned him to the bed.

The room was dim and smelled faintly of Icy Hot. But aside from the mussed bed, everything was neat.

"You don't need to use your doctor voice on me," Adam said.

His spoke slowly and his voice seemed mild, but she could still feel the sting in the words. "You don't seem very surprised to see me like this," he added as he lowered himself gingerly onto the mattress and unbuckled a knee brace. "I guess you watched the game."

She hesitated, not sure how much to tell him. She leaned over and started arranging his system of ice packs. "I saw it. I was in the arena."

A pause. He turned his face away from her a little. "Guess you got your money's worth then."

She tightened her fists. "Do you have any pain medicine?"

"Stop doctoring me," he snapped. Then softer, "I'd like a moment with my girlfriend, not with a medical professional."

She couldn't help herself, she wanted to say. At least she understood pain medications. Yes, the wounds were superficial. Yes, he was probably fine, although peevish. She sat down next to him, and his arm came up to caress her butt and waist. His touch slid up her arms, to her hands, and he loosened her fingers from their tight hold one by one. *He's right. Relax*, she told herself. *You've waited for this all week.*

She toed off her shoes and eased herself down so that her head rested on his arm. His sheets were wet and cold from the condensation of the cool packs. The rest of her was not really touching him, but at least she was near him. It had been so long. She closed her eyes and breathed him in.

"Come closer," he said. "I'm not going to break."

He pulled her in. "Be careful," she said.

"Damn it, Helen. I've missed you and need you to touch me, and I don't want you to be scared."

"I'm not."

"I know it looked bad on the ice. I was aggressive tonight – I had a stupid argument with Molotov – and the other team responded. Damn it, I was planning on having you come to a game after the vote on the arena. I was hoping to clear things away tonight and finally have good news for you. But I look like a mess."

She prodded him gently. "What good news?"

She saw the gleam of his smile in the dim light, and she felt a twang of something that was almost like relief. *He could smile.* That was enough to make her happy, and she tipped her head up and beamed right back up at him. "I found acceptances from grad schools waiting for me tonight," he said.

"That's great!"

"Plus, I've already been learning the ropes with Molotov's West Coast operations. And the way things are going, I might be able to play for another year or two with the Wolves."

Helen stiffened but Adam continued. "Now that my family's farm is on more stable ground, it would give me the opportunity to save up a little. Plus, I've already checked and I can defer enrollment in the programs I applied to – it'll give me time to make up some of the credits they want me to have." His arm tightened around her. "This is mostly good news. Finally, I have opportunities. I have choices."

Helen took one breath. Then another. "You're going to play for another year or two."

"It's early to say, but… I didn't think I'd get to this point. I didn't think I'd survive. It's not always going to be like tonight, Helen. They actually want me to play. They want me to do something that I *know* how to do. I'll get paid."

Although she knew it was technically impossible, she could actually feel her heart tearing away from the spot in her chest and dropping down to her stomach as he confirmed it. Her mind flashed to the sight of him earlier this evening, his face contorted and bleeding. He'd raised his head, almost seeming to look toward her, almost as if he'd exit the fray and come to her, and at that moment, she'd felt a wild, desperate hope. And then he'd turned, and his fist had come up and he was in the fight again.

"Tonight was rough," he was saying, stroking her hair as if she were the one who was injured, as if she needed soothing. "But come on, it wasn't that bad. I know it's a lot to process, Helen. But can't you see how relieved I am? It's good news for me."

"You sound happy," Helen said, low.

"Well, I guess it's hard for me to get my mind around it, too. But overall, it's a good thing, right?" He sighed. "We should sleep on it."

He lipped her neck and shoulder and started to unbutton her sweater. And she wanted him to do it. She wanted to do it again – to fall into him and just let him take over. She wanted to depend on him, but she just couldn't. He was injured, and she couldn't – shouldn't – lean on him.

"Adam," she said, "what if I don't want you to play another year?"

"It's not that bad," he said.

"It isn't nothing," she said, her voice breaking a little.

"Are we at that point, where you can ask me to alter my plans? We've never even gone out on a date in public."

"Yes and no. Maybe. Of course I think of a future with you. I wish it were now."

"But why isn't it, Helen? The arena vote is going to be here soon, and after that… why aren't we planning beyond a few days together at a time?"

"You're right, we should sleep. You're hurt."

"I'm not that hurt, Helen. You're a physician. You know these are things I'll heal from. The thing you're really afraid of is that one day, I'll end up like your father and that you'll have to take care of me."

"I love you, Adam. I love you this way – well, less banged up. Whole."

She couldn't help the gulping sob that came out of her throat this time.

"We don't know what will happen, Helen. Things could change. We could find treatments. But I saw how you looked at me when you came in tonight. You just… you shut down everything, as if you couldn't deal with me. The only way you could get yourself to touch me was like a doctor. But Helen, if you treat me like this now – if you treat me like a patient, like a case study, like a problem, through most of the relationship – well, what's the point? I love you, Helen. I love you whole. I love the fact that you were an amazing young teenager and that you're gorgeous and amazing now. I love the fact you'll change, and I want to get to see it. But I'm starting to think that that's not going to happen. With us. Because I change all the time, too. I've gotten to the point where I've had to deal with my failure – my fear – and I am moving on. There's hope for me, Helen. I have these opportunities in front of me, and sure, they scare me. But I recognize them for what they are, and they give me strength that's been really hard won. And now all it takes is that look on your face to blow a huge hole in it.

"I need more from you, Helen. I need some kind of commitment – not that you'll endorse the arena, not that you'll be photographed coming out of a club kissing me. Just… I want to call you my girlfriend, to go out to a movie like a normal couple, to just hold your hand and meet your friends and have you meet mine. I need you to say that you'll be there for me. That I can come home to you. That you can come home to me and not be afraid that one day I'll lose my memory, that I'll die slowly."

She found it hard to breathe, as if every part of her was shutting down, as if her throat and stomach were swamped by the helpless anger that had been sitting inside her since her father's diagnosis. "Do you know what it's like for me, Adam? To see you get hit? Do you know what it's like for me, knowing what I know?"

"When it comes down to it, how much more do you know than anyone else? That it can happen? I know it, too. That it will? You have no idea and neither do I. The difference is that you've told yourself that you need to do something about it – find a cure, prevent everyone from ever getting hit, stop all the hurt. But Helen, for right now, you can't stop anything."

"I can't accept that."

She flinched from the deceptive solidity of his arm, of his chest. She sat up. Everything about her felt shaky. Her hands were probably trembling. She rubbed her arms.

"You're leaving," he said. "Again."

His face was in shadow.

"Yeah, I am."

She didn't move. Maybe he would change his mind.

But he turned his face away.

"Fine, Helen. Go. But don't ask me to give up a chance at a future when you can't even stand to be in the same room with me for this night."

Chapter Twenty

This time, Helen really couldn't find her car.

Adam had insisted on calling her a cab to take her home last night. He even sat with her to wait for it – he on one section of his long couch and she stiffly on another – because that was the way he was. It was uncomfortable and terrible, and yet as she sank in the cab, she was grateful for that stupid annoying decency of his. And that realization made her heart wrench even more.

Now, she was wandering around Adam's apartment building in the dark and quiet of an early winter morning, looking for the familiar shape of her hatchback. She hadn't been able to sleep in the night, and she felt numb, as if she'd screamed herself hoarse and deafened herself, too. As if her muscles had tensed so long that she'd forgotten how to move them. She would find herself stopped in front of a truck, an SUV – a vehicle that did not remotely resemble hers – because she couldn't see through her tears. She couldn't even lift her hands to her face to brush them away.

After what must have been an hour spent circling the area around Adam's building, Helen gave up and went back to the office. It was still early, but Petra was already there making coffee. Not wanting to talk to her friend, she grabbed a cup and shut herself in her office until her first patients arrived. Unfortunately, she'd scheduled them late so when Sarah breezed in without knocking, her friend caught her staring dull-eyed at the wall.

"Did you really bike in?" Sarah asked. "It's too damn cold for that today."

"I can't find my car."

Sarah snorted. "Typical Helen."

Helen tried to laugh but failed. "I looked for a while, then gave up."

"Where'd you leave it?"

"Not far from here," Helen said.

"Maybe it was stolen," Joanie offered from the doorway. "We got a flyer from the precinct about an uptick in car thefts in the neighborhood."

At Sarah's urging, they spent their lunch break driving around the neighborhood looking for it. It was definitely gone. Petra accompanied Helen to the police station to file a report and called the insurance company.

Helen let herself sink back into her friends' efficiency. She let Sarah put her and her bike into Sarah's car. She didn't argue when Sarah turned on her GPS. "I can't decide if you're less upset about this than you should be or more upset," Sarah said.

Helen didn't respond.

She got through the rest of that night. In the morning, Petra drove her to pick up a rental car. But when she slid into the hatchback and turned the ignition, the radio blared to life, preset to a sports call-in show. Within seconds, Adam's voice — instantly recognizable yet oddly sonorous because of the deep bass of the car's stereo system — surrounded her. At this volume, she heard his breaths, the sound of his tongue against his lips as his mouth moved to make words. She could feel the vibrations of his voice through the seat. She closed her eyes and let the pleasure-pain of hearing him seep deep into her.

"I thought you'd be right behind me," Petra said when Helen arrived at the office.

Helen shrugged and looked down. She knew Petra was eyeing her.

She didn't think. She worked. She rode her bike, ran, and did yoga. She let her thoughts rest delicately on the line above the memory of her last few days. The awareness was always there, but she didn't allow herself to remember. When she couldn't sleep, she dosed herself with pills.

If anyone had noticed how quiet she was for the rest of the workweek, they didn't say anything. Maybe they thought it was the trauma of the theft.

Her mom made her talk to her dad on Sunday night. Oddly, the silence between their sentences was not as fraught this time. She had no energy to keep up a stream of chatter between his slow, thick speech, and the grief numbed her against the sound of his difficult swallowing.

She told him a little about the cases she'd seen that week, as she usually did. In the middle of it, he asked, "Why are you sad?"

"I— my relationship isn't working out," she said.

"Why not?"

"I keep imagining losing him," she said. "And it scares me."

Of course there was a long pause while Harry Frobisher worked through her words. Or maybe he hadn't even understood them. She sighed. "It was good talking to you, Dad," she said, getting ready to hang up.

"Helen," he said, his voice suddenly clear.

She could almost hear the fighter he'd once been. "Yes, Daddy?"

"Don't be afraid of losing."

–

By early Sunday evening, Adam had received a phone call from his sad manager, Bobby, who said that there was growing interest in him from a few East Coast teams. Bobby sounded excited. Energized. "Keep this up, and you may have a chance of big success next year," he yelped.

Adam should have been excited, too.

More options yawned in front of him, huge and dark and empty. He flipped through his graduate school acceptance letters again. Portland State wanted him to earn more credits before admitting him to the school of social work. In San Diego, he'd be plunged right into the psych program. He'd have a fresh start. He could surf and run in the sand. He'd refashion himself as a California boy. No more hockey, no more skating. No one would know who he was.

Well, there would always be people who knew him. Helen, for one.

He hadn't made any decisions yet. *If* the team managed to do well, *if* he continued on his streak, then sticking with hockey for another year at least would probably be the most sensible choice, moneywise. Above all, he was sensible Adam Magnus, Minnesota farm boy.

Sensible and alone.

To avoid hurting his knee, he'd been wearing his brace religiously and working his core and his arms. And he listened to choral music. Helen's gift had started him on it. Now Bach's Mass in B Minor lived alongside Black Sabbath's "Spiral Architect." The wrath of God section from Verdi's Requiem accompanied him on the treadmill. Angels and seraphim sang him to sleep – when he could sleep. Right now he was supposed to get some rest. He stretched himself in his bed, naked, his earbuds buried deep in his head, a mask over his eyes, an ice pack strapped around his knee. He'd taken some Tylenol. He'd rubbed cream on his muscles. He smelled like an old man, but anyone looking at the wires and packs attached to him would probably think he was a creature of science fiction. If he ever did earn big money, he should buy a traveling hyperbaric chamber. Yevgeny Molotov probably had one.

Helen had once told him that someone had made up the "fact" that people only used about ten percent of their brain, that the rest of it was submerged in some sort of gelatinous liquid of possibility. In reality, all areas of the brain fired and returned shots, functioning with the others. Damaging one part of the brain affected another. Every part had a function; every part was connected to the other.

She had been lying on top of his chest, he remembered, her fingers mapping his skull as if she were feeling all synapses zapping in his brain. When her restless body shifted, she would knead his thigh muscles in increasingly glorious and uncomfortable ways. But he hadn't rolled her to his side. He hadn't wanted to move. So he had gritted his teeth and watched her through half-closed eyes, until finally her hands had walked down his nose and lips, down his chest, and to the dark places between them.

He couldn't go there now. It was too painful.

The arena vote was soon. Despite the anti-Yevgeny campaign, it looked like the billionaire would win. Adam would win. He should be happy that he was a man of possibilities. He could put off major decisions for another year or two. Maybe he could stretch it out even longer, give himself more time, more money.

He must have fallen asleep because when his phone rang, he jerked up and sent his ice packs flying. He glanced at the screen. It was Serge. "We need to talk."

–

"I'm retiring, Adam. I wanted you to hear it first."

Adam sat heavily in the hospital chair, careful to keep his leg straight. He'd left his brace at home.

Serge began to laugh. "Look at us old men with our trick knees."

Serge gave his offending limb a pat. "ACL tear with MCL strain."

His voice was tight but clear. Certain. Adam shook his head, trying to understand. "What happened?"

"It wasn't feeling good after... the game the other night."

"After the brawl," Adam said, flatly.

"Right. But I ignored it."

"Serge."

"Hey, we all play through pain. And this wasn't new or different. So then I maybe overdid it during practice."

"But you never—"

"I never overdo it during practice?" Serge laughed. "True. That's why I've lasted so long. But, you know, we've been doing well lately. And I felt like I had something to prove. We've all felt that way lately. But I just had a little swelling. Iced right away. The physio told me to take it easy. I had a good weekend. Slept. Watched some tape. Normal things. And then this morning, I almost knocked my brand new iPhone off the breakfast bar. I swiveled off my stool to catch it goalie-style, knocked my knee against the corner just as my foot came down, and my knee torqued. I heard a pop. And well, that was it. I was on the floor. Caught the phone, though."

Serge grinned, then grimaced. "Betrayed by technology," he said with a shrug.

Adam shook his head slowly. He still couldn't grasp it. "You can come back after a ligament injury."

But Serge had his jaw set. He shook his head. "I've been thinking about it all day while they've been assessing me. Those orthopedic surgeons and team docs, they told me I'd need surgery. I can *tell* it's bad, Adam. They'll have to operate. It will be months of rehab to just get myself back into shape. And then, to get it to the point where I can drop down to my knees or stay in a squat? The team's only begun to recover. I think it's time, Adam."

Adam got up and sat down again, but he was beginning to realize that he wasn't going to convince Serge. Another voice was asking him why he was so intent on it, when he himself had been willing to give up just a month or two ago. Serge was his best friend. They'd started out together, and Serge had been there when the drinking had gotten bad and when recovery seemed worse. "Give it a day or two, Serge. Let the drugs wear off. Have you talked to Bobby?"

"Bobby? Are you kidding? I'm letting you know now, then I'm telling my parents. Then, *after* they give me the next dose of drugs, I'll tell Bobby and let him screech and wail and he can break it to the team. I've got this planned out."

"I just don't understand," Adam said, even as understanding began to dawn on him. "You were so set on playing until you couldn't anymore. You were upset that I was thinking of getting out."

Serge considered a moment. "Well, now that I'm resigned to it, it doesn't seem so bad." He said, more quietly, "I was envious, you know, when you started talking about retiring. You had a university degree. You had a doctor girlfriend. You had possibilities. I just had hockey and more hockey. And the hockey I had – well, we were a shitty team. All I had for the future was blowing all my savings, then serving poutine to tourists at my parents' restaurant. But we pulled the team out of a slump – I mean, the season is still long and we're still low in the standings. It's a small step, but I feel happy about what we have done and I still love the game. It's a good way to end when you think like that."

They were quiet for another moment.

"I don't love it anymore," Adam said.

"I know. But I don't understand why you are still playing?"

"Money."

"Hah. I guess that's another reason. But you have enough, don't you?"

"I don't know."

Serge shrugged. "Listen, Adam. I've known you for a long time. Unless you are spending all your cash on fancy scarves – and that is a possibility – then you probably have enough if you are sensible. And you are. And with wealth, well, you can save and save, but you get to a point and you can't plan. Anything can happen. All of the stocks and banks in America could go under. You don't know the future, and you can't live like the worst will happen. You have no idea what will happen."

"That's what I told Helen," Adam said, slowly. "I told her the difference between her and me was that she thought she had to do something, to prevent the worst from happening. For her, it was dementia, and for me… I guess it's money."

"See? You are a pretty smart guy. Now, do you want to sit here while I make my phone calls? I might need your help with Bobby."

"Huh? Yeah, sure." Adam nodded absently. His mind was still reeling after all of the blows he'd been dealt in the last hour. But the worst one was the one he'd dealt himself.

Chapter Twenty-One

Janel had brought in a group of new interns, and Serge's retirement was their first major press conference. The room buzzed with their young energy. Now, they were throwing out ideas to make Molotov more palatable.

"Maybe if Molotov were a kinky billionaire, people would like him more. People love those," a pale, blonde intern was saying.

"Only in books, dumbass. It's not going to win over legislators," countered her buddy.

"Well, it should."

Serge and Janel were huddled together in a corner, their heads practically touching, as they went over what Serge was going to say. Janel had seized on it as an opportunity to talk about the vote without actually talking about the vote. Bobby had flown in from LA overnight and was under strict orders to be quiet. He was pacifying himself with multiple cups of coffee.

Adam leaned against a wall, surveying the room. He supposed he could join the interns. He was one of them – albeit better compensated. But he was learning the ropes, just the same.

Still, he needed a moment.

After leaving Serge at the hospital, he hadn't been able to sleep.

He'd gone through all of his options again, going through all the permutations and possibilities. But mostly, he'd paced in the dark, his steps slow and uneven as he favored his sore knee. He stared out the big window of his apartment, staring at the lights of the other buildings, down, down at the elusive glimmer of the Willamette. And he thought of Helen and how scared she had been for him and how much she did love him to be so hurt when he was hurt. She'd been scared for him, and he hadn't given her any reason to not be scared.

They drove to a hotel where Janel had arranged for the reporters to meet them. The place was bristling with microphones. They shuttled quickly to an office and shut the door. Janel had instructed Adam to wear a suit. He also had a brace on over his trousers today, partly out of solidarity to Serge. Why bother hiding it, anyway. Janel had tried to fluff his hair, but Adam batted her hands away. Serge got to wear whatever he wanted. His dark blue jacket matched his own proudly displayed brace, and he'd wrapped his crutches in navy hockey tape. He let Janel smooth his shoulders, and he sent Adam a wink when Janel started to fiddle with his coif.

Adam rolled his eyes, dug his phone out of his pocket, and scrolled through a long list of messages. Of course, Helen hadn't called. Why would she after what he'd said, after what he'd demanded? It seemed so reasonable at the time to expect her to want security, but he had been the one asking her to wait for him – to worry too much for him. Clearly, he could do enough worrying for both of them. She had been looking out for him, in her own way. But had he been looking out for her?

His stomach roiled as he followed the others into the press room. His best friend wouldn't be on the road with him. He was playing a game he didn't like and working for a man he loathed. And he didn't have Helen. Sure, he'd have some semblance of security, but what exactly was he trying to preserve?

Janel had been going over the basics, and now it was Serge's turn in the spotlight. He started off by thanking the team, the coaches, his family. He even managed to acknowledge Molotov International, although his huge smirk at the end was probably going to elicit a few questions.

"I want to take a moment to thank my teammate and my friend, the best guy I know, Adam Magnus. Sometimes in this game, it seems like we're just a bunch of guys trying to bash each other's brains out—"

Janel flinched.

"But the most important thing I've learned from Adam here," Serge continued serenely, "is that who you are on the ice – who people *think* you are – doesn't have to be all that you are in life. The ice is just the surface we play on. So despite the fact that my career ended before I thought it would, I'm looking forward to my retirement. I'm looking forward to the rest of my life. Thank you."

A small silence followed Serge's words. God, was he getting choked up? Serge stumped over and gave him a half hug. Then he gestured down at their matching knee braces, and the reporters laughed and took pictures, and the room buzzed as journalists started asking questions.

Adam wasn't sure when exactly it was that he sensed Helen. But he found himself turning her way before he could question why, and there she was, almost hidden behind a pillar at the back of the room. And her eyes were on him.

Janel was answering a question at length and hadn't noticed, but Serge had seen her and he grinned at Adam then gave him a nod. No one would miss him.

Adam excused himself from his seat and walked carefully around the periphery of the room, partly because he was afraid that if he moved faster, the dream would dissipate. When he reached her, he could see she was pale and worried. Her eyes darted searchingly across his face, as if she couldn't believe he was there. She had dark circles under her eyes, and her fingers clasped and unclasped as she gazed up at him. She'd never looked better. He put his hands on hers – her hands so alive with muscle and nervous energy – and held them gently. And behind the pillar, to the whir and flash of cameras, her face began to lighten with relief as he reached down and kissed her.

Chapter Twenty-Two

"I'm sorry," she said as soon as the door to Adam's apartment closed behind them.

"You know, I was never really sure you were Canadian. You don't like hockey, and you don't generally apologize. But the way you say *I'm sore-y*, now I'm positive."

This was good right? He was teasing her, his eyes warm and… relieved?

They'd run out of the conference room together, through to the lobby, to the street. It was pouring outside, and they were both soaked through by the time they managed to find a cab.

She shivered, and they stared at each other.

"Towels," he said. "I should get towels. And something hot to drink. Then we talk. But for the record, I'm sorry, too."

They stared at each other for another moment. Then he went off to the closet, and she headed for the kitchen, leaving a trail of water behind her.

"Would you rather have Ginger Jamz or Peppermint Posset?" she called, surveying his cabinets.

"You're making me drink herbal tea?"

"You're the one with the collection."

He came up behind her and rubbed her hair gently with the towel. He moved down to her shoulders, her breasts, and back. Then he handed her the towel and moved away carefully. "I'll go get us some clothing to change into," he said, looking down at his ruined suit.

She took a deep breath and stifled her disappointment. Maybe he wasn't ready to be with her. Maybe he wanted to tell her that he was moving to another team? That he was running off with Serge to Yukon territory to pan for gold? But why would he bundle her out of the hotel and bring her here if it was over? Unless he was just going to hand her the things she'd left in his apartment. That's why she was here: She was going to receive a shoebox filled with torn underwear and old issues of the *New England Journal of Medicine* and a toothbrush.

She brought the tea out to the living room and found a pile of dry clothing on the couch. Quickly, she stripped off her wet things, donned a huge sweatshirt, and went to put her stuff in the dryer. It looked like Adam was going to be stuck with her for at least half an hour.

When she came back, he was stretched out on the couch with his leg propped up and he was holding the tea.

She cleared her throat and sat down on the opposite end.

"I've talked to my supervisor, Weber, about changing my focus and joining the research on parkinsonism at the hospital. I thought it would be a – uh – more productive way of using my energy. I'm also going to get counseling."

She paused. "I gave up on my dad too early – or maybe in the wrong ways. I was so focused on myself and my feelings. Maybe I need someone who can just listen to me vent and worry. And with the research, maybe I'll make a difference this way. But even if I don't, I have to live with it. So, I'm doing this for me because I need to, but I'm also hoping that – well, I'm also doing it for us. If there is an us anymore."

Adam nodded, still staring at his mug. Helen held her breath.

"Helen, I love you. I don't want a life without you. I've decided that I'm going to finish out this season and keep working with Janel, learning the business side. She's made noises about quitting Molotov, starting her own firm. I was thinking of asking her if I could join. And I'm going to go to school part time. Now that you're here – that we're here together – I know that it's the right decision.

"I thought about playing more because I liked the idea of going out with a better record. For so long in my life, I was focused on it. I liked the idea of showing people I was some kind of winner – showing you."

"Adam."

"It's hard to get out of that way of thinking, you know. It's hard to assume that not everyone believes that. But when it came down to it, the game hasn't been the same for me. The travel is getting to me. Serge is gone. I'm taking longer to heal from injuries."

"The other night when I saw you, you were really good," she said, her tears clogging her throat. "It was powerful. But you're right, even though I could admit that you were good, it's not how I think. You don't need to win that kind of game for me. There's no shame in changing your mind about what you want to do in life. You never needed to redeem yourself."

He shrugged. "I know that now. But I worry because money and fame and success are knotted together for me, and I'm just beginning to untie it. I don't want to be one of those guys who blow through their earnings the minute they stop playing. I've met those guys. So I think of the future, too. I worry – not the same way you do, but it's there. But maybe I need to trust you to keep me grounded."

"You can trust yourself to keep you grounded," she said softly.

"We need each other," he said. "That's become clearer and clearer to me. I need you to be around. I want to start a new life, and sometimes that's going to be weird for me. But I want you to be my constant."

He looked up from his side of the sofa and their eyes held, but he still hadn't touched her.

Lightning slashed the room, followed by the crack and boom of thunder. They both turned to the window, and Helen released herself to walk toward the violent sheets of water. "We should talk more," she said.

They needed to. But she couldn't – not just yet, not right now while they still believed in each other. Her whole body felt heavy with all the apologies and kisses and love she needed to drop on him, and she was afraid it would burst out in a messy torrent, unintelligible. She clenched her fists.

"People will be able to see you," Adam murmured, coming up behind her again.

"No one will see us in this rain," she said, turning and slipping her palms down his back.

She traced every muscled ridge back to his stomach. She wriggled her fingers through his wiry chest hair and plucked gently at the tiny curls, admiring how they sprang back. He was beautiful, but so human and so warm. She leaned toward him and rubbed her cheek on him, and she felt his arms come around her.

She was not going to move; they were going to stay right here. She was not going to let him go anywhere. Not while she was alive. And right now, she felt the blood rushing through her veins, the bass beat of her heart, and the trilling of her pulse. She felt her nerve endings twanging, and she knew she was going to fight tonight – with him and with herself.

He stripped the sweatshirt off of her and threw it down to the floor. But with his body rubbing against hers, his hands rubbing her naked back, touching her flanks and smoothing her belly, she felt so warm. She tipped her head back, and his hot mouth descended on hers.

He backed her to the window, and as soon as her back touched the cold glass, she cringed forward into him. He put one warm hand between her and the surface and, with the other, gripped her breast.

They were kissing each other with their eyes open. She didn't want to look away from him. She loved seeing the shock of his dark pupils against his icy irises, his careful, slow blink as her hand, and tongue, and body slid over his surfaces.

Another lightning strike and another crash of thunder filled them. He pressed her against the glass again, and she almost screamed at the cold on her ass and shoulder blades.

Her pulse was racing, from the stimulation of his fingers, from the chill of the window, from the crash of water as the rain continued to pound behind her. It felt dangerous and uncomfortable and arousing all at the same time. He hoisted her more firmly this time and entered her in a deep thrust that she felt up her ribs and spine, almost up to her throat, and she finally closed her eyes just as another crackle of lightning and thunder tore through the air.

They were not smooth or pretty. Within minutes, her back began to warm; the mixture of condensation and sweat made her thighs slide dangerously on his hips. It was precarious, but it also pushed him deeper into her, and she felt him tighten his grip. His eyes looked wild, but she was not going to fall, not while he held her. He was searching her face as if trying to find confirmation that she was with him. She was. She hissed and adjusted her slippery legs around him, changing the angle, changing the pressure, and she bucked against him with everything in her, choking and gasping his name.

He was silent, as if concentrating on the pleasure coming from her body to his, his to hers, on standing and holding her and keeping her body in his embrace. The glass was going to crack under the force of his pounding. Someone on the street below or in the opposite buildings would see their wild fucking outlined by the lightning. Or the storm would strike the building, earthquakes would rumble. They would plunge down into the cold, wet night, and they would still be wracked with joy. They would go, screaming each other's names, but she was beyond caring.

She gave a final cry as he spasmed into her, his torso suddenly wild with strength.

She felt herself sliding, sliding down as he flooded her with a hot rush, and her body kept pulling him in, drinking him.

She closed her eyes. For several moments, there was nothing except the rain and the darkness and their sticky, aching limbs.

They were on the floor, his head against her breasts, her legs tangled under his arms. "Come on," he said after a long while. "Let's get some ice, and then let's go to bed."

"Damn it, your knee," she said, scrambling up to help him as he moved himself gingerly.

"I feel great," he said.

Later, while they lay in bed, Adam asked her why she'd been at the press conference. Helen thought, then laughed. "Serge called my office. He said that when — *when* — I talked about him to you in the future, I was to refer to him as the Love Coach. What's that about?"

Adam laughed. "That's Serge's idea of a second career."

He kissed her and laughed, and it was a beautiful sound. "I guess we'll both be pretty busy with these new roles."

He started to run his hands down her back. His nose was in her hair. His breath tickled her neck, and it was the best feeling in the world.

"Maybe we could think about moving in together," she said. "You know, maximize our time. Save money."

"You sweet talker," he said.

"I just want us to keep the sex window."

"Is that what we're calling it now? Sex window?"

"It seems appropriate, if a bit on the nose."

She kissed him on that appendage. But he looked serious. "So to be clear, even though I went off about how I want to be with you and even though we're talking about this big step, things are going to be changing for me and I'm going to have to ask you to let me figure things out for a while."

"In case you haven't noticed, I don't exactly have it together over here, either." Her eyes filled with unexpected tears. Again. To cover them up, she ducked and kissed his hard shoulder, his jaw. "Are you wearing Icy Hot?" She sniffled. "That stuff is spicy."

She rubbed her forehead against his chest.

"Sure, it is. You know, for someone who's such a hard driver, you're also kind of weepy."

"I'm going to sob all over one of your jazzy scarves if you aren't careful."

He held her close.

"So we're really doing this. Together," she said, her voice muffled.

He swallowed and touched his lips to her hair. "Yeah."

286

"You know we're all wrong for each other."

"So you've said."

She nodded. "As long as you know."

Acknowledgments

This book (and my previous one!) would not exist without the efforts the sharp, dedicated, and frighteningly efficient folks at Crimson: Jessica Verdi, Tara Gelsomino, and Julie Sturgeon.

Galois Cohen, you'll never know how much I appreciate your willingness to slog through those early stages with me. To my husband, thank you for putting up with my inability to wield commas correctly.

And all the lovely Toasties who answered my questions, shared your smarts, and gave unstintingly your support, you've changed my life.